About the Author

William Pruitt was born in Florida but raised in a single-parent household between Michigan and Kentucky. His college years were spent surrounded by the hills of the Daniel Boone National Forest, attending Morehead State University. When he's not working on his stories, he's engaging with the world around him, whether with his friends and family or on his own.

Mafia Magnate

William Pruitt

Mafia Magnate

Vanguard Press

A CIP catalogue record for this title is
available from the British Library.

ISBN 978 1 83794 057 8

Vanguard Press is an imprint of
Pegasus Elliot Mackenzie Publishers Ltd.
www.pegasuspublishers.com

First Published in 2024

Vanguard Press
Sheraton House Castle Park
Cambridge England

Printed & Bound in Great Britain

To Christian, Isaac, Jaden and Dylan

Chapter 1

The sun was just setting across the Manhattan skyline when Devon Gregory walked into his penthouse apartment, lighting it in an iridescent pink glow. The full wall windows allowed for the light to cast through the entire apartment, carried by the white walls down the hallways and into the darker crevices. He sat the small box of belongings on the glass-topped, steel-framed desk, from which he could watch over the whole city.

"So, Phoenix Security officially closed the doors of the New York regional office, huh?" Victoria, his beautiful wife, asks from the kitchen.

"Yeah. Mr. Callehann came by personally to offer me a job overseeing national, and possibly international, operations. However, I just felt led down a different path," Devon responds, pouring himself a glass of Irish whiskey, as he sits on the steel mantle surrounding the fireplace separating his living room and his open office.

"Really? Thinking about going back to teaching maybe?" Victoria says, peeking around the corner.

"Not particularly, and I doubt Adelphi wants me back."

"I was thinking more, NYU. I heard from a colleague that they need a new doctoral history professor to head up their department."

He was staring at the roaring flames in the glass chamber, watching them flare and flicker into the air, dancing with their flashes of orange-red color as he thought of teaching at New York University. Suddenly there was a loud ringing that resounded through the apartment that pulled him from his thoughts. Devon grabbed the handset off his desk.

"Hello?" he asks, walking over to the window.

"Devon, it's Antonin Maretelli. I have some news to talk to you about."

"It's good to hear from you Antonin, but right now isn't the best time."

"Oh, sorry to hear that. What's happened since we met in college?"

"Well, I left college sophomore year to join the army, after a few years in the infantry division, I was asked to join the Rangers. After a couple years with them, I was recruited to join the Special Forces division of the US military. I retired from that, against their wishes after four or so years as the commander of one of the forces. Then I finished my teaching degree and taught at a private boarding school here in New York, one of the best in the nation. While teaching, I finished writing, and published a few books. When the school found out that I was in a relationship with another teacher there, they forced us to choose between ending our relationship or one of us leaving. I chose to leave because she loved teaching there, then I joined a paramilitary security corporation, rose through the ranks to become a regional operations commander, overseeing operations for the Midwest region of the US from the New York office. Until the company lost all its US accounts and closed the division. So today I cleared out my office and I'm starting the next phase of my life."

"Oh, I'm sorry that you're out of work now, Devon, but good outlook on the situation and I might be able to help you define that next stage."

"How so?"

"Well I've also been busy for the past two decades, I became an alderman for the city of Denver, Colorado. The next election I ran for mayor, and won. After that term I became a representative for my district, then senator. I'm currently waiting for my campaign manager to set up a press conference for me to announce my intention to run for governor of Colorado. During all that, I received a call from grandmother a couple days ago, She lives in Sicily now and thought I could help."

"So where do I come in?"

"She's what's called the *capo di tutti i capi*—"

"Boss of all bosses?" Devon states, remembering research from one of his books. Victoria looks over from the desk momentarily, where she's emptying the box, before heading to their bedroom to get ready for bed.

"Yeah, she leads the Cupola, you know, international governing body for the Italian mob. They ran into a problem with the Commission here. The Commission which is the collective governing body for the American Cosa Nostra, or Mafia, including the Five Families of New York and the Chicago Outfit."

"I don't want to sound rude, but I know. I've had to work with one of the families in New York when working for the security company, they ran a protection racket on the company, so I've worked with them."

"All right, so you're acquainted with them. Well anyway, the Commission has stopped contacting the Cupola, and that only happens when they try to make a power grab on the international circuit. So, G-Ma called and asked me to rally a group of trusted individuals to get the attention of the Commission."

"She wants you to get their attention?"

"Yeah. My first thought was getting the old crew together and starting a family to place ourselves on the board."

"I would agree but we'll need to make adjustments."

"Well let's discuss that in person, want to meet up in Lexington, KY?"

"Sure. Let's meet next week with the crew that we know for sure are able."

"All right, see you then."

After getting off the phone, Devon checked his email and nearly collapsed. In his inbox was an email from a covert US email server that informed military groups of new assignments. He opened the email and saw that it included his service photo with the letters LAL, meaning 'liability, acutely lethal', stamped across his photo. As soon as he recovers from the shock he grabs three bags, he'd prepared for when this moment came.

"Vic, we need to leave now. I got the service termination email."

"The what?" she says walking out of the bedroom in a robe with curlers in her hair, looking at the computer. "Oh. The email, all right." She rushes after him.

Devon follows her out of the apartment, initializing the advanced security system he personally reengineered.

"Who was on the phone and why were you mentioning Mafia terms?" she asks as she gets in the Toyota Corolla registered under her mother's maiden name.

"I'll tell you on the way," Devon says, shutting the door, and climbing into the driver's side. "We'll really need to thank your mom next Christmas."

The next week, Devon pulls into the parking lot at Malone's. He slips out of his Chevrolet Tahoe, also registered in his mother-in-law's maiden name, and walks into the restaurant, he scans the restaurant, and sees the sleek black hair which is unmistakably his Italian associate. He tells the hostess that there should be a reservation under Maretelli or Gregory with one of the parties already having arrived. As soon as she finds the name on her list, she crosses it off and escorts him to the booth where his friends were awaiting him. Antonin and Sean were sitting talking about all the crazy things that'd happened since they last saw each other. As he approaches, Sean is the first to see him and greets him with a firm grip, followed soon by Antonin. Then they sit and once Antonin finishes his story, Devon asks what Sean has been up to and why he's the only one to come meet him. After leaving college after freshman year, Sean Gallagher had worked as a front desk clerk for Holiday Inn in Atlanta, Georgia, progressing up to be the hotel manager.

When Antonin told the story in person, Devon understood the seriousness of the matter. the Cupola was the top of the line for the Italians, if you're in with them, you've reached the top, so it's best to stay on their side and if the Commission had aggravated them, then the best course of action was to side with the Cupola. Devon was all for it, especially after the LAL email. Since he'd need all the protection he could get, Sean wasn't so convinced.

"Why put my life as it is at risk? I mean I'm not living the best life I could, but I'm living fairly decently."

"Damn, things really must've changed in your life, the Sean I knew in college wouldn't stop and be settled at fairly decent. He would've strived until they get what they deserved," Devon says.

"I'm being realistic, Dev. You're talking about challenging the biggest and toughest men in the country."

"That's what they want people to think, they're no better than any of us. Perception is key and because of the past and with the backing of the Cupola, the Commission have been perceived by the American public to be untouchable. The thing is they're under a whole new regime now: Garmaggio, Horatio, Verratti, Corlani, and Gorgio. All bosses that were unheard of three years ago, now lead the Commission and have lost the support of the Cupola," Antonin states.

"So, what you're trying to say is—" Sean begins.

"They're no different than we are, the only difference is they have inherited a system they barely know. Not only do I have contacts that can understand it, we would be creating ours and know it because we'd make it," Devon adds.

"Fine, but if this goes south, I want full amnesty in the fallout," Sean says, giving in.

"Fair enough. I'll take the full fall for everything," Devon states, gaining a glance from Antonin. "Hell, if this doesn't work I'm dead anyway," he adds, explaining the events following the phone call.

Then it was time to discuss who else to recruit to the cause—to start a family, per Cupola tradition—Antonin needed two more individuals to join the cause. The group decided on Aaron Jacobs and Xavier Jones. Two of their college friends they figured would go along with the Mafia thing.

Devon was placed in charge of contacting them. They were fully willing to at least entertain the idea but needed assurance that it was legit. Therefore, Devon set up another meet-up at his apartment in New York in two weeks.

Chapter 2

Devon met all four of his guests at Newark Liberty International Airport, having just arrived from his safe house in Minnesota. Once they had all their luggage, Devon drove them to his penthouse apartment and invited them to entertain themselves in the private theater. As soon as they were settled, Devon prepared the snacks.

As he was about to pick up the bowls of snacks, a faint ding and a soft clink caught his attention. Knowing full well what that meant, he put the bowls down quietly and pressed a button on the remote in his pocket, automatically locking the theater. He then pressed another button beneath the island counter in his immaculate kitchen. The countertop rises and the wall beside the fridge slides out. Revealing a hidden wall compartment concealing a full set of combat armor: chest piece, arms, legs, boots, and SAP gloves. Under the counter, in a clandestine locker, was an assortment of weapons, from smoke grenades and machine guns to katanas and throwing knives. Devon fully outfitted himself in the armor and weaponry before pressing the button again and concealing the hidden spaces.

As soon as they clicked shut, the door was bashed in and the windows shattered with soldiers flying in. Devon quickly tossed smoke grenades throughout the house, unsheathed his katanas that were crossed across his back and began his assault on the window breach team. He did one of the traditional poses with katanas, one raised horizontally above his head.

As he exited the pose, walking toward his now open windows, he slashed one across the chest to his right, then to his left, turning as he slashed the second assailant to make sure the first wouldn't fall out of the building. As he was about to strike the last window assailant, he heard someone approach from behind, so he kicked the final assailant, spinning to slash the approaching assailant and stopped just short of the now kneeling assailant's jugular. He then raised his sword and hit the assailant with the hilt of the blade.

He then moved briskly toward the living quarters, dropping his katanas on the way and unsheathing his daggers, before being met by a barrage of fire as he came around the fireplace. He moved his blades swiftly, deflecting every shot. He then sheathed them and replaced them with his dual pistols. As he approached the position of the first ground assailant, he shot him in the shoulder and then jabbed him with the butt of the gun. Then he took a defensive position behind the bust of Alexander the Great, from there he shot rounds at the soldiers in positions two and three. Recognizing their styles, he knew these were two of the operatives he chose to recruit to Delta

Force and could pinpoint their weak spots. He took them down without a second thought and moved up. If he counted right, that left only one, and knowing the protocol like he did, having written the new ones for the team, he knew that only the commander was left and as he knew how the team worked, that meant it was his former expeditionary officer (XO), Lieutenant Colonel Travis Carson Richards, TC for short.

"So, it's Colonel Richards now, huh TC?" he says, baiting his former second in command to reveal himself.

"Yeah, it is Dev," he says rounding the corner. "How'd I know it'd come to this?"

"I led this force for three years, I know most of the men on this team, besides the one brought up to take my spot. I know the fighting style of most of these guys, and I rewrote the training protocols for the team," Devon responds. "Didn't think about that when selecting the team did you?" he asks, holstering his pistols.

"You wouldn't—"

"No, of course not. None of them are dead, or mortally wounded, a little time in the med bay and they'll be back to top notch. So, what are you going to do TC, kill me?" Devon says, walking toward the bar to get a glass of whiskey.

"Well that's my only option so—" Colonel Richards answers matter-of-factly, training his pistol on Devon's chest, directly at his heart.

"Now wait a minute. There's always more than one option, I taught you that. Let's think here. You can always return and say you couldn't take me down. I decimated the whole squadron and you barely escaped with your life."

"You know the rules, don't come back until the job is done. If I returned without a body, and without a team, I'd be discharged for sure," he says, shooting the glass Devon was filling.

"Exactly, haven't you had enough of the elite forces? I spent three years leading this team and left, and it still took me just as long to start living again. I have a wife, an expecting wife, waiting for me at a cottage in Colorado. I've published books, taught school, and worked for the private sector and I'm living the good life, without the excitement and terror of the elite forces. Join me," he says, fixing another glass and an extra for his former XO, offering it to him.

"Join your what, what is there to join? I lost my family, my wife in Corinth is all I have left," Richards says, forcing the glass out of his reach with the pistol he still had aimed at his former CO.

"Then join her, quit this ridiculous unit and let others take up the gauntlet, we've served our country enough. Let the younger, more suited people take it over now," Devon asks, raising the glass again.

"Fine, but we'll need to make it look like I at least put up a fight," TC concedes, accepting the glass and taking a few sips before placing it on the mantle next to Devon's.

"One more spar for old time's sake then," Devon says, putting his glass down and retaking his position.

Devon releases his weapons harness, removes all his armor, and leaves himself with only one USMC Ka-Bar knife. TC did the same and only had the same, the same knife as well. It was the knife issued to them as an award from their former CO in the army.

They circle around and TC makes the first move, lunging forward at Devon, who parries the lunge and slashes at TC. The tip of the blade barely scratches TC, ripping his shirt and making a thin cut on his chest. In retaliation, TC comes forward with a blizzard of slashes, most being parried by Devon. However, a few make contact and Devon comes out of it with a few scratches on his arms and chest. As he pulls back, TC lunges and Devon wraps his arm around TC's wrist, pulls TC's arm under his own and twists TC's hand. This makes TC effectively drop the knife. As soon as the knife is on the ground, Devon kicks it away while releasing TC and placing his own knife on the ground and kicking it away as well. It's time to finish the sparring. They circle each other, waiting for the other to strike, yet again TC is first, advancing to tackle Devon. Devon effectively locks his feet into their current position and withstands the tackle. Then he swings his body around, so he's behind TC, and swipes at his feet. TC, caught off guard, is tripped and flips over landing on his back. He is quick to jump to his feet and throw multiple punches, Devon is swift to dodge the first few but TC makes contact on the last couple. Devon responds with a flurry of hits of his own and lands most on his combatant.

After that, Devon successfully brings TC to the ground, and with that TC taps out, exhausted.

"Damn, Dev, you still got it, six years later."

"You know, I might've left the service but training never quit. I got a whole room by the theater, which reminds me, until your comrades wake up, I'd like to introduce you to a few of my friends," Devon responds, offering his hand to his former XO.

"Ah. All right. Show the way," Richards replies, grabbing his friend's forearm and pulling himself up.

Devon escorts TC to the theater, unlocks and opens the door, which pauses the movie.

"Guys, I'd like you to meet Colonel Travis Carson Richards, excuse me, former Colonel Travis Carson Richards, I'm entertaining him to join us as a member of my detail. When we return, I'd like for all of us to get to know him and hopefully persuade him, as well as Aaron and Xavier to join us in this endeavor."

Devon then leads TC back out to the living areas, where the Delta Force team was rousing from their injuries.

"You mind telling them the plan?"

"Certainly. DELTA ONE, LISTEN UP! We have been asked by High Command to go on discharge indefinitely. I will be spending this time with Colonel Devon Gregory, our, FORMER target; he bested us, so we show him that respect. You all are welcome to join us, if not you can accept a permanent change of station back to Fort Liberty."

"Sir, under whose authority was his file cleared?" states the newest addition to the team.

"Mine, and as the commanding officer of Delta Force, I have the authority to restrict any, and/or, all of you to post if you are to disobey this order. Please await further instructions in the training room three doors down on your right."

"Yes sir!" rings out from the GIs as they walked, and limped, to the specified room, clutching their bodies in pain.

Devon then escorted TC to the living room, which had sustained only minimal damage in the brawl. After sitting him down he retrieved their drinks, and the other members of his guest party, and revealed the hidden selection of liquors from within the antique globe to them, motioning them to pick their poison.

As he sits down and offers everyone a cigar, he starts explaining what's happened since he left the service.

"So, the night you all were sent the mission brief for my manhunt, I was just getting off the phone with Antonin who presented an interesting opportunity, that Sean and myself have agreed to pursue, and we are trying to get Aaron and Xavier to go along with us on this. Form a Mafia family to usurp the Commission here in New York, under orders from the Cupola in Sicily," Devon says, speeding through that last part.

"Wow! Interesting, where would I come in?" TC wonders.

"You'd be my lead enforcer."

"Basically, your private security. Great, back under your thumb!" he replies, with sarcasm and loathing under his tongue.

"No, you'd be vested with all authority you now have and you would accompany me to family meetings and be my right-hand man in all matters."

"What matters are you in charge of?"

"We have yet to work that out."

"I'm down with that, just make sure I get the gentlemen's industry!" Xavier interrupts, with a wide grin.

"So, you're down Xavier. TC? Aaron?"

"Sure. What do I have to lose? I go in for knee surgery tomorrow, Suzanne's love of dancing keeps dislocating it to the point that they need to do surgery now," Aaron says with a hint of bitter distaste in his voice.

"Why the hell not? You screwed my return to the military anyway," TC states.

"You know you missed me. It'll be like old times again succeeding together," Devon says, clapping TC on the shoulder.

"Yeah but I was always behind the great Devon Gregory. You always got the best recognition!" TC grumbles, brushing Devon's hand away.

"You really think that? Of all people, you should know I didn't do it for the recognition, and if I knew it meant that much to you, I would've stepped down and let you take command. You know that!"

"I know, but it doesn't matter anymore. Let's hammer out these details so I can dismiss my men," he says, taking a long sip of his drink.

"All right," Devon responds.

After a couple of hours of discussion, and a few glasses of whiskey, it was decided that Devon 'The Don' Gregory would run the operations involving arms trafficking, nuclear weapons smuggling, military equipment smuggling, assassinations, bombings, loansharking and people smuggling. He also received responsibility for coordinating enforcers and security forces for the Mafia. Antonin 'Kingpin' Maretelli was given charge of political corruption, money laundering, blackmailing, forgery of identification, passport fraud, counterfeiting, economic espionage and identity theft. He was also placed in charge of facilitating the bases of operations for the other bosses. Sean 'Snakes' Gallagher was placed in control of hijacking cargo, stolen goods, car theft, art theft, jewelry theft, bank robbery, burglary, antiquities smuggling, oil smuggling, insurance fraud and stock fraud. He also oversaw providing vehicles for transportation, which Devon's crew would improve upon to verify its safety for use. Aaron 'Dagger' Jacobs would supervise all individuals working in the areas of drug trafficking, bootlegging, fencing, kidnapping, copyright infringement, computer hacking, organ trafficking and price fixing. He would also be responsible for tracking disablement; he'd make sure the Mafia couldn't be followed and would clear any evidence that the families were present. Xavier 'Bullet' Jones would run prostitution, gambling, embezzlement, point shaving, bankruptcy fraud, credit card fraud, securities fraud and cheap labor circles. He'd maintain the Mafia's economic standing by assisting Aaron and Antonin in clearing records of major economic activity.

After hammering out all the details of who runs what, the group decides that meetings will be called once a month, with no regularity and the time and place would be sent out via call or email. After discussing that, Devon escorts all but TC out, since he and TC have a few more details to hammer out before the night closes. Once everyone else is gone, Devon escorts his friend into the office to discuss their cover operation.

"As you can tell by the activities we'll be involved in, the jobs we're going to be doing will not be upheld by any legal means. Therefore, we need to discuss our cover operation. With both of our former careers being in the military, I feel the easiest conversion would be to do a private sector security firm. With you being the lead of this former Delta team, we could bring them in as the first caporegimes and soldiers of the Gregorian crime family, we could place several of them on the board and use the others as our first operational team of the company. What do you think?"

"Doesn't really matter what I think now does it? You're the boss." TC responds disdainfully.

"No, of course it matters what you think, you and whoever my consigliere will be are going to be my two closest advisers and I want your advice on this."

"Fine, I think it's a good idea on paper, but we'll need more than the fifteen guys in that room to start a security firm, especially if you're taking a few to the board. I can reach out to some of the guys from other special mission units, who are about to leave, when I go in to report my loss and receive my exit from service."

"All right, I can contact a few guys from when we were in the infantry division and Rangers. All right, now that we got that figured out we need to figure out a name and the departments."

"What about Triskelion?"

"Triskelion? Where'd you get that from?"

"It's been a symbol of motion, sometimes equality, and in Christian terms, eternity and a symbol of the triune nature of God."

"I like it. Triskelion Security Corporation. We'll need at least four departments in the firm to provide all the security: personnel, systems, equipment and vehicles," Devon determines.

"We'll also need the traditional business departments like research and development, finance, human resources, production (operations management) and marketing."

"Of course, so I'm going to place you in charge of creating it, all right?"

"Sure. I'll come to you when I need the details of everything. I can probably snatch a few weapons and armor stuff from Fort Liberty when I am discharged," TC agrees.

"You got a lot riding on being dismissed, if you don't get discharged, and just reassigned, that could be a potential exploitation for us to use."

"Right, but I doubt I'll just get reassigned for failing to apprehend a high value target like you." TC states adamantly.

"What if you did apprehend me though, we could use that as a rally cry for those that want to leave the special forces and give you another set of hands to get a hold of resources?"

"How would we walk out of Fort Liberty though?"

"Simple, disgrace High Command."

"High Command has been in control for years. How are you going to disgrace them?"

"Get me in there and I'll show you." Devon states confidently.

"Fair enough, let's deal with the first situation we have beforehand though."

"What's that?"

"The Delta Force team waiting in your training room? Don't tell me you forgot."

"Ah, of course not. Yes, let's!"

Devon and TC then made their way to the training room in the apartment. When they entered the room, all the soldiers were exercising.

"ATTENTION! Commanding officer is present," informs the first soldier who noticed their presence.

"I've ceded command of this regiment to Colonel Devon Gregory, from this point forward you all are no longer in the service of the US military directly, you are within a contract of the newly created Triskelion Security Corporation run by Colonel Gregory here. I've signed a contract placing us under his direct command immediately. We will still work within the United States Military Special Operations Division, but only under the terms of the contract I've signed us to. If you do not like this, you can be effectively restricted to post at Fort Liberty immediately, but once done, there is no coming back. Would anyone like to inquire about this privately with Col. Gregory?"

Several soldiers raised their hands. Devon directed them to make their way to the second door on the left from their current position. As soon as they were in the room and the door was shut, Devon turned to TC. "Hold my shirt please!" Devon then removes his plain white button down, revealing a white sleeveless beneath.

Devon walks into the room he designated earlier, and a few minutes later, three of the five officers to inquire returned, consenting to the contract, another followed soon after, looking a little more battered than the others, followed shortly by Col. Gregory.

"Where's the fifth?" TC wonders, handing Devon his shirt and a white towel.

"He chose not to consent and has been dealt with accordingly," Devon says, wiping his bloodied hands with the towel and replacing his button down over his newly replaced undershirt. "Ruined my favorite workout shirt too."

"Ah, you can bleach it," TC states casually, " Anyone else want to inquire privately?"

Of course, no hands went up after seeing the bruised and bullied faces of the four that had already done so.

"Very well. In the morning, we will be returning to Fort Liberty. Our purpose for returning is to bring Col. Gregory in for detainment, which is a cover mission. While there you are tasked with retrieving arms, armor, vehicles, and other necessities to be brought back after our permanent change of station. Only certain people will be tasked for doing such, but you all are to be aware so that you can assist our men in retrieving such. Am I clear?"

"Sir, yes, sir!" they respond.

"At ease. We depart at zero nine hundred hours."

Devon and TC walk out of the training room. Devon then takes TC to see the soldier who refused to consent to show how the enemies of the Gregorian family would be handled.

As the door swung open, a chair was revealed, surrounded by small pools of blood. At the feet of the chair lay the body of a soldier in uniform with his shirt removed. He was laying face down.

"You didn't?"

"How many times do we have to go through this? No. After he passed out, I injected him with a powerful neurotoxin that will erase his memories from the past eighteen hours."

"He'll remember everything about the raid on your place?"

"Up to where I took him out in the first assault, you'll have to explain to him that you were able to detain me and so on. We can't use him for the team, so we'll just leave him at base."

"As you say, boss," TC says, looking at Devon with a smile.

Chapter 3

The next week, TC pulls a Humvee into the Fort Liberty vehicle depot. In the Humvee with him are two of his forces and a cuffed Devon Gregory. As they pull the vehicle up in front of High Command, TC grabs hold of Devon's arm and gives the illusion of dragging him inside. Once inside, TC relaxes his grip.

"Sorry, sir."

"You're fine. You were upholding the illusion of my detainment. Now let's get to the meeting chamber."

TC escorts Devon through corridors until they reach the office of High Command. Upon entering the room, Devon and TC are greeted with an assembled body of generals from special operations commanding generals to the joint chiefs of staff representative. TC escorts Devon to the seat situated in the middle of the room, before the panel of generals. After sitting him down, TC backs up and stands behind Devon.

"Former Colonel Devon Gregory you have been brought before this military council at your own request. Accordingly, you are awarded a time to speak, please make your appeal as to why you MUST, as you put it, be removed from our liability list and released from our custody?" Vice Chairman of the Joint Chiefs of Staff Harrison Donahue, inquires.

"Certainly, Vice Chairman," Devon states, rising to his feet. "As this present body knows, about fifteen years ago another colonel in command of a tier one unit retired against the wishes of his superiors. Vice Chairman, I'm sure you remember well, since you were in command of Special Forces then. Anyway, a similar situation happened, after several years off the service, a detachment was sent to 'take care of' this liability. The problem was he knew the training of those dispatched and could disarm all the forces you sent. He sent the severed hands of all the operators back with their Ka-Bar knife in their hand and atop the knife, their insignia patch. You let him go without chasing him again. Colonel Howard Josephs hasn't been on the radar since. The only difference in this scenario is that I left your men alive. Ask Colonel Richards, I took everyone out and could've killed him if I needed to."

"Is this true, Colonel?" the commander of Special Forces wonders.

"Yes, sir, sadly it is," TC responds, as expected.

"So, what does that matter? You are in our custody now."

"Actually, you are at my mercy, Colonel." TC steps up and removes the cuffs, several staff flee and the assembled generals jump back in their seats.

"Colonel, restrain him, what is the meaning of this?"

"Now I command Colonel Richards and the entire team you sent to my apartment as well as several inside sympathizers who agree with me. Here's how this is going to work." Devon starts walking around the room, rubbing his wrists as TC walks and places a packet before Commander George Bastron. "Colonel Richards just placed before you a contract, upon signing that contract you will relinquish control of forty-five percent of the forces in this fort to my command as well as all the weapons, ammunition, and armor that can fit in fifteen Humvees and three Chinook helicopters. If you don't sign, I take the best fifteen percent of your forces here and all the equipment and vehicles listed regardless. If you sign, I'm willing to allow you to use the forces you sign over at your discretion for an allotment of three years. Make no moves on me and my associates, and block any government attempt to do the same, and I'll uphold my end. Understood?"

"We really have no choice in the matter. Guards!" the commanding general proclaims, with a squad of guards falling in immediately.

"TC!" Devon responds without hesitation.

At which point TC tosses Devon two pistols and they come back to back as the squad surrounds them. "General, you know just as well that we shoot fast and accurately enough to eliminate this entire squad, and as much as I don't want to do that to these brave men, I will if I must," Devon exclaims, locking eyes with the vice chairman.

"At ease! Very well, you can have the troops. Commander, sign the paper, I'll sign it as well," Donahue declares.

"I wouldn't do that, if the commander signs, it relinquishes control of forty-five percent of all Special Forces, if you do, that's forty-five percent of all United States military forces. I might have taken advantage of this opportunity, but I'm not trying to control the whole military."

"Very well. Colonel Richards, here you are. Best of luck to you. How are we to know which ones you'll take?"

"I'm leaving with fifteen percent of all the forces present, the rest can stay and follow your directives, until otherwise notified by myself," Devon explains.

"As you say. Good day Colonel Gregory." He nods to the cunning commander, with all due respect.

"Good day, generals," Devon says as he turns away from them.

TC and Devon walk out of the room followed by the squad of guards, and as they move across the fort to the vehicle depot, ten more squads join their forces and approach the waiting Humvees, as the three Chinooks hover above, filled with ammunition, weapons, and armor. Devon looks back toward the command center of Fort Liberty as he climbs into the lead Humvee, smiles and ducks his head into the passenger side of the vehicle as TC laughs and gets into the driver's seat and heads off the convoy as it takes off through the North Carolina countryside.

They arrive at the space that Antonin had bought for their start-up operation. The Chinooks landed in the large field across from the building, the Humvees all parked in the large lot behind the building, as the soldiers exited the vehicles. TC and his team began directing them to unload the equipment and begin cataloging it, before taking it into the warehouse attached to the side of the building, already labeled as Triskelion Security Corporation. Devon walks into the office part of the building and selects the office with the window into the warehouse, where tables lined the walls and ladders rose to numerous levels of storage, on the ground floor was enough room to store ten Humvees.

TC revealed all the whistles of the building, upgraded for their use. Devon was surprised to see rotating storage cabinets, retractable landing platforms, and multi-level parking, as a ramp revealed itself at the pull of a lever, at which point the Humvees were taken down to the parking garage, the landing platform that retracted into the roof extended and the parking lot dropped to reveal two more platforms. The Chinooks took to the stations and the two descended down into the sublevel hangar while one remained on the platform above. All the while the soldiers kept cataloging and moving ammunition crates, weapons caches and cabinets of armor.

Devon was stunned at the building and decided that TC was to run the everyday operations of the security company while Devon began to place their other stakes of the family work, only five soldiers were told of the Mafia's existence and their role in it, one was chosen as caporegime and given authority to contact TC when necessary. After placing TC in command of the security corporation, Devon ordered one of the soldiers to take him back to his apartment, which had been repaired while he was gone.

He walked in to be ambushed by his wife and the German shepherd dogs they'd adopted while at their safe houses. They were former military dogs trained by both the military and law enforcement to find threats and take down assailants. After weeks around Devon and Victoria, the dogs were starting to acclimatize to the new lifestyle and their new owners. As Devon sat down at his desk, the alpha male, Horrus, took to his feet and relaxed there, while the beta female stuck by Victoria in the kitchen. The other three dogs in the troop were relaxing in their beds near the wall by the door. Then the phone rang, all the dogs perked their ears and stood, facing the phone, until Devon picked it up.

"Yeah?"

"Dev, it's TC, just wanted to let you know all the equipment's been cataloged and stored, the last Chinook is going into the hangar, and I'm sending the operators to the barracks beneath as well. I'm leaving five here to guard the place and bringing six with me there to guard you all."

"Actually, just bring five with you and leave six. Also, only bring one other guard inside with you, the dogs barely know you, we'll need to acclimatize them to the entire detail at some point so that they'll know who to trust and who not to."

"Very well. Headed that way in two Humvees now."

"Oh, and TC, be cautious, we're on the radar now."

After Devon hung up, he placed the phone back on the receiver and went to the kitchen.

"Who was that dear?"

"TC, you know how I told you about that Mafia thing Antonin and I discussed?"

"The one I advised not to get involved with but you did anyway? Yes, I remember."

"Hey, that Mafia business allowed us to get those beloved canines that you adore so much, and anyway, TC is a former friend who is now my enforcer for the Mafia and as such he's my chief security personnel. He's bringing five guards from our first Mafia work and wanted to warn us. I told him to only bring one in with him, because of the dogs. They've run   into TC a couple times, but they need to get acquainted with the whole detail eventually. So, we'll have one by the car, two outside, by the elevator, one down by the entrance to the building, and one inside with TC. I'll have the one inside, stay by the door, but TC will be posted outside of the bedroom at night so no need to worry about them bothering us when we want to be alone."

"You know that isn't happening in a while, we've got our child on the way."

"I know, but this guard thing is for the next phase of our lives, and as soon as the doctor clears it, you can bet you're jumping back on this horse!"

"Shut up!" she responds, hitting his chest and plunging a spoon of delicious chili into his mouth. "How does it taste?"

"Oh, ah, ha, ha, ha, hot, temperature wise, but other than that perfect. I'll check the cornbread," Devon says, fanning his mouth and making his way to the double ovens.

"Already done, it's cooling in the first top oven."

"Then I'll check and make sure you didn't poison it," he says, opening the door and reaching in.

"Oh no you don't, if I wanted you dead, I'd be much more obvious, and we have guests coming. And they will be eating, no questions asked, Devon Jacob Gregory!"

She slaps his hand with the bamboo spoon she was using to stir the chili. He snaps his hand back, as she points it at him finishing her statement.

"Yes ma'am, Victoria Francesca Alvarez Gregory. Jeez, I hate that your name is so long and mine sounds like your talking to multiple people," he says, fanning his hand to rid the sting from the hit.

"Ah, the burdens we bear," she says, getting bowls, saucers, and spoons out.

"Indeed," Devon responds laughing, loving it when they have a weirdly loving conversation like this.

As Victoria starts dishing the chili into four bowls, a knock sounds on the door. Devon walks around the dogs, all watching the door as he answers it, letting TC and the other guard in.

"Gentlemen, this is my beautiful wife, Victoria. She's an English teacher at the Adelphi Academy of Brooklyn. She's also an amazing cook and soon to be a glorious mother," Devon says, snatching a piece of cornbread, as she takes them from the pan and onto a platter, and placing his hands on her stomach as he stands behind her.

"Now that's enough praise, Devon, I'm sure these gentlemen are hungry, please join us for dinner," Victoria says, kissing Devon's cheek.

They sat down and enjoyed the delightfully delicious chili. After two servings, Victoria reveals that she also made banana pudding. As she set it down on the table TC heard chatter on his earpiece, after a second he turned to Devon.

"Sir, there's a man claiming to know you waiting by the elevator. Were you expecting anyone else?"

"No. TC come with me, Horrus, come!" Devon responds, getting up and heading out the door.

When their alpha was ordered about, the other dogs took up position around Victoria and the former Delta Force operative positioned himself by the wall. Devon walked to the elevator where he was met by two of his former Delta Force team. Behind them they had detained a man in military uniform wearing a green beret. Devon smiled, and looked to TC, motioning his hand away, a signal to release him.

"Lieutenant Colonel Conner Fiore, battalion commander for the United States Army Special Forces Division, codenamed Green Berets. Long time, no see," Devon expresses and pulls him in, giving him a firm grip.

"Colonel Devon Gregory, same. How's Delta Force?"

"I left the service six years ago, TC here, was the former commander of the team. Colonel Travis Carson Richards."

"I remember TC from when we were all in Rangers together. So how is the team, Colonel Richards?"

"Recently received new orders to follow Colonel Gregory's directives and perform as his protection detail."

"So those are your Rangers downstairs, I got past them without a word, not sure why it didn't work here."

"These are Delta Force, downstairs was just Rangers, but I'll take your advice into consideration," TC states strictly.

"Enough posturing, you two. Lieutenant Colonel, please join us for dessert and we can talk afterwards."

"Very well, Colonel, but can you put the canine at ease?"

"Ah yes, Horrus, enough!" he says, balling his hand at his side.

Devon then escorts the men back to the apartment where he gets another bowl for Conner. After introducing him to Victoria as a military acquaintance, he whispers in her ear, "Potential underboss."

Victoria gives everyone a moderate serving, while Devon got an excessive one, due to his love of the dessert.

Small talk between everyone was quite common as they enjoyed several servings of the fabulous pudding until most of it was gone. After taking care of everyone's dishes and placing them in the sink, Victoria began to empty the leftovers into plastic ware.

"Gentlemen, if you would be so kind as to await me in the living room while I help the missus," Devon says, getting up.

"Certainly," TC and Conner respond.

TC instructs the security guard to take up a post by the door, before he makes his way to the living room, followed soon by Conner. In the meanwhile, Devon walks over to the sink and turns on the hot water, rinsing all the dishes before placing them in the dishwasher.

"Gentlemen feel free to help yourself to some drinks," Devon calls out, then he turns to his wife, grabs the now empty chili pot and places it in the sink while rinsing it with hot water. "Dinner was fantastic, baby," he says, kissing her.

"Thanks, hun, I enjoyed having your guests over. It's nice to only fill a medium plastic container instead of a couple big ones."

"Good. Now do you want to join us in the living room or are you going to go entertain yourself in your art room?" he asks, as he places the last few dishes into their dishwasher.

"I'll go to the art room, leave you boys to handle business. Love you!"

"All right babe. Love you!" Devon says, giving her a kiss as she walks away.

He fills the detergent pocket, closes the dishwasher, and starts the cycle. Then he makes his way into the living room where he finds his guests talking over glasses of Irish whiskey. Grabbing a glass of his own, he sits in his leather wing chair, at which point Horrus comes to rest by his feet again.

"Conner, I'm glad you showed up, I was just about to call you. How's the Green Berets treating you?"

"Not too good, actually. I just came up for review by the board and I don't see it going well, I actually haven't done my job as precisely as they wanted."

"I'm sorry to hear that, but it might be how things are supposed to turn out. You remember Antonin from college?"

"How could I forget? He fluttered about as busy as a bee."

"He did, well he's been given an interesting opportunity with his grandma—"

"The one from the Mafia?"

"Yes, that one. She runs the Cupola now, the Sicilian Mafia commission, that oversees global Mafia activity. They lost contact with the Commission here in New York and asked Antonin to form a "family" to gain their attention and help get the Cupola back into the loop on the Commission."

"What does this have to do with you and me?"

"I've joined this family as a boss, TC is my enforcer, and I'd like to offer you the position of underboss."

"What does that mean for me?"

"You'd have absolute control over my section of Mafia operations. I'd be the only one above you."

"What about TC?"

"You'd work alongside him; he's in charge of running the security details for the entire Mafia but under my directives."

"All right, I'm in."

"Good, your first assignment is to recruit as many Green Berets as possible to join you as well as acquiring arms for use by the security forces. TC and I will accompany you to your hearing."

"All right. What benefits do I get for this?"

"All of them. Security, money, everything. I'm receiving five thousand dollars a week from the Cupola, you'll receive slightly less, three thousand five hundred dollars. TC is receiving two thousand five hundred dollars a week, as will my consigliere, who I'm meeting to persuade to join us in two weeks."

The next day, the three mafioso leave, with Horrus and one of his betas, for Fort Liberty. They pull in and slide out of the redesigned Humvees, which are now black with a white triskelion on the front doors and on the bull bars as well. As they walked down the street, a select brigade of men saluted Devon and TC as they passed and made their way to the command center.

Upon entering, they were escorted to the room where Devon had been investigated and there sat the same assembly of generals and officers.

"Colonel Gregory, your presence is not required. Please leave."

"I go where I please and I'm no longer under your command so therefore you have no place to give me orders."

"I will not take that disrespect! Guards!" the vice chairman of the joint chiefs exclaimed. However, this time the guards did not come.

"Do you not remember my last visit? You gave forty-five percent of the forces here to me, that means any forces to cross into Fort Liberty, even the new ones that the vice chairman sent after I left."

The chairman turned away, clearly infuriated by the fact that he was bested. "Anyway, Lieutenant Colonel Fiore, you have been brought before this board of review on the basis that you are using unconventional methods to complete the objectives of the United States Army Special Forces. This isn't the first time this has been brought up either. Therefore, this board has already approved your dismissal. Good day Lieutenant Colonel."

"Hold on Vice Chairman, I believe the Lieutenant Colonel has something to say," Devon speaks up.

"I request, no demand, that if I am to be discharged from the service, that I want twenty percent of the forces here to be discharged with me."

"You're crossing boundaries and making demands that aren't yours to make."

"Correct Vice Chairman, they are demands that are mine to make. Lieutenant Colonel Conner Fiore recently signed with Triskelion Security Corporation, and was immediately placed on the board as CFO. Giving him authority to make demands for more soldiers. However, let me make this clear, since my last audience before you, I've earned quite the reputation among the troops, offering better benefits. You already see that the guards no longer respond to you when I'm present so you know the extent of my power already. I'm not taking all your troops; I'm leaving you with thirty-five percent of all troops in this fort alone. I have yet to move to other forts. Cooperate and I won't need to."

"Fine, contract?"

"TC, give it to them." TC approaches with a contract, and after getting the signature, returns to Devon's side.
"Thank you, good day." Devon, TC, and Conner all turn and begin to exit. "Oh, and that also gave me power to take medical supplies and another three Chinooks, five jeeps, two MR.APs, two Stryker ICVs, thirty AWDs, one Flyer-72 ALSV and one JLTV. Thanks for the corvette ships, frigates, and submarines, as well as the drones."

Devon then walks out as the generals all look at each other in astonishment and Conner gets the brigade together and apprehends the goods. Devon hops onto one of the AWDs instead of the Humvee this time and rides off out of Fort Liberty followed by most of the fort's troops.

Chapter 4

A few weeks later. Devon was having dinner with Xavier at Jones' casino. While Devon was at work with TC, everyone else got their enterprises underway as well. The Cupola was the one ultimately responsible for the start-ups , so Antonin's grandma sent Cupola representatives to personally secure the properties the day after everyone left Devon's.

"So, how's it going? The business I mean."

"Oh, so far so good, I only have the gambling and prostitution rings operational but my underboss, Trevor, is working on securing the others. Darren, my adviser, is keeping up with him while Cole here maintains the operations of the casino and prostitution business, as my enforcer he also thinks he has to be right up on me, like within fifteen feet at all times. Can you do something about this?"

"I'll alert TC to contact Antonin, and the other bosses to get the enforcers together for proper security parameters and training."

"Thanks."

"No problem." As soon as the words leave his mouth, his phone goes off. "Ah, excuse me." Xavier nods in understanding.

"Hello?"

"Sir, it's Conner down at the office, we have a little problem."

"What is it, OG?"

"There's a troop of well-dressed soldiers here, who say they work for the Garmaggio family. They also say their boss is coming in a few minutes."

"I'll be there right away OG, they don't leave." Devon hangs up the phone and gets up. "TC, let's go. Thanks for dinner, Bullet, but we have a problem to deal with at the office. I'll have Victoria call you to set up a dinner at our place, and tell Celina she's invited too."

"Will do. Good luck."

"I won't need it, they will," Devon says as he puts his fedora on and grabs his umbrella.

Devon and TC pull up to the office five minutes later. Surrounding the building are ten cars, all black as obsidian. Devon passes through them and walks into his building to be met with machine guns in his face.

"Don Garmaggio, let's be civil about this."

"Colonel Gregory, you're back but this is much lower than our last meeting."

"You know that the company shut down their regional HQ and I couldn't leave the area, so don't try rubbing salt into a wound that isn't there."

"Fine. Men outside, Francois and Armando stay."

"That's better," Devon says as most of the well-dressed soldiers walk past him.

Devon walks across the room and glances out the window into the warehouse, where his forces are slowly amassing.

"Don Cesare Garmaggio, why don't you go by your real name, Colonel Howard Josephs? Afraid the service will come after you again."

"I've never been afraid, Devon, you know what I did to those fools who tried to take me down. I was just rising in the ranks then. Now I run things, I don't have to answer to you."

"You're right, you don't, but you made one mistake when you left, that I chose not to repeat when I did. I took Delta Force operators with me, oh and a Green Beret. TC, OG!"

At that point the two men disarmed and restrained the Italian enforcers, and as Garmaggio was about to say something, Triskelion forces burst through the door, and placed a barrel to his head.

"You see Garmaggio, I know you can handle yourself, but I also know you have compassion for those you work beside and above, like these individuals with no special operations training. So, we're going to negotiate." Devon nods, and TC and OG place the two mobsters in chairs while soldiers restrained them there. Once restrained they were gagged.

"OG, hold my fedora. TC, here's my shirt and tie," Devon says handing the men the things.

He then jabs both men in the gut.

"Now Cesare, you came to exercise a protection racket on us, right?"

"I'm not saying a damn word," the boss says defiantly.

Devon smiles. "Bad choice." He then unveils a knife, and stabs Armando in the leg.

"Yes! I came to exercise a protection racket for the Commission," he claims as his enforcer tries to shriek in pain.

"Good, and why?"

"I'm not that stupid, you might be wired," the boss says firmly.

Devon then twists the knife in Armando's leg. "Really?"

"To assert the control of the Commission," he confesses seeing his enforcers' faces contort in pain.

"We aren't going along with that."

"You have no choice in the matter, Colonel," he says smugly.

Devon shakes his head at the don, and moves the knife into Francois's leg, immediately twisting it. "I think we do."

"Fine, we won't collect the racket on you, for now," Cesare says.

"That's not good enough, Josephs," he says, removing the knife and slashing the shoulder of both enforcers.

"Fine, fine. We won't collect the protection rackets from Triskelion Security Corporation. Better?" the boss begs through the screams of the enforcers, admitting defeat.

"For now." Devon tosses the knife on the counter. "But let's show you what will happen if you harass any of my officers and associates, I know you have a list somewhere."

Devon then grabs his umbrella and beats both enforcers beyond recognition. "Is this clear enough, Don Cesare Garmaggio?"

"Yes," he says. TC releases him from the restraints. "However I'll warn you, you just earned the right to be watched by the Commission," Garmaggio says, trying to pull his last string of intimidation.

"I'll return the favor," Devon says, whispering into his ear. "The Cupola has eyes on you all now as well so don't bring your men back unannounced again."

Garmaggio looks at Devon in shock.

"Oh, and if you are wondering why your men never came in during the screaming it's probably because the fifty plus elite soldiers that are pinning them down and the arsenal of Humvees surrounding them. And from now on you can call me Devon 'The Don' Gregory of the Gregorian crime family under the authority of the *capo di tutti i capi*."

Devon smiles as the head of the most powerful crime family walks out followed by his two brutalized enforcers, limping. As soon as they are out of view, Devon has TC call Antonin.

"Antonin, it's Devon. We're out to the Commission!" Devon says walking out into the middle of the field.

"What do you mean we're out?"

"The Garmaggio boss paid a personal visit to our start-up location and tried to enforce a protection racket. I was able to clear all our families of the racket, but he said we're being watched by them, so I retorted that they're being watched by the Cupola, they may not know we're working with the Cupola, but they know the Cupola has eyes in the city."

"Oh Dio! That's not good. Luckily the votes were released last night and I won the race for governor of Arizona, and Sean and Aaron say things are going well. I assume you're doing fine. How's Xavier?"

"He's set up his secondary location making final preparations to move to Florida, he has Trevor starting his other operations but has two going now. TC and OG are setting up our first deals for arms and coordinating our other jobs. So, if you all on that end are clear, I think we are OK with being revealed. Not ideal but not in a bad spot. Xavier plans on moving his base of operations when things get underway."

"Yeah Sean is going to Missouri and Aaron is setting up in the California mountainside. I guess we are good to go. Need anything else?"

"I will also need you to send me the names of the enforcers, advisers, and underbosses for everyone so I can provide accurate protection details and have all the enforcers contact TC, they need to be properly trained in protective service."

"Right. Got it. Blessings. Bye."

"Bye, Antonin," Devon says, then emails Sean about the types of vehicles he's getting for everyone and asks him to have them brought to the start-up address.

The following day, as Devon went to the office, he saw an influx of guards on the property.

"TC, what's with the extra guards?"

"The visit last night got a lot of the soldiers worried, so much so our capo took the liberty to establish a perimeter guard, and sniper posts."

"Well take care of it, the Mafia is an accepted organization, but it's an underground one. All these guards will make local authorities suspicious of our motives and we don't need them tailing us, especially with the Commission watching us."

"Yes, sir."

He disappears around the side of the building, while Devon makes his way inside and to his office. Upon entering his office, he meets OG, waiting for him. The underboss immediately knew to state his business, so he informed Devon that their connections on the black market for guns and guards was established and that Devon's name was out and about the bounty hunter realm as being of utmost character, but to really gain any more ground with those circles, they'll need to make a show of efficiency and control. To that end, OG was securing a list of high value targets that would get the attention of both contractors and assassins. Also, the crime families in Portugal, Japan, Mexico, Morocco and Canada had all been contacted to get their men involved in smuggling. OG, with the help of Cupola contacts, acquired a port to use for shipping internationally. He was also able to pay off port authority workers and the local sheriff's office, to secure their lines for minimum detractions. After informing Devon of all his activities, he was dismissed with orders to oversee smuggling efforts, from packaging, to arrival and transport, all aspects of the process. Also, he asked him to select members for positions of capo, who would be brought before Devon to be evaluated.

After OG left, Devon opened his email to find several emails for Adriana Acerbi, the younger daughter of Carmine Acerbi, international CEO and Cupola boss. She informs him of several contracts for assassination, low key to other hunters but helpful for establishing a reputation. Devon looks through them and says he'll see what kind of team they could assemble. His email also contained a message from Antonin stating the date, time, and location of the first official meeting of their family. Denver, Colorado in three weeks' time at Devon's ski lodge. At that time all operations need to be underway. Luckily for Devon they were, but he still had lots to do. He had to acquire the cars and modify them, finish the redesign of the recent vehicles acquired from Fort Liberty, execute these assassination orders he just received from a Cupola boss, and establish himself with the local community as a benefactor to them, and not a detriment.

The priority was the Cupola assassinations. So, when TC got back from his conversation with their oblivious capo, Devon had him assemble a team of top notch sharpshooters and hand to hand combatants to manage the assassinations. Then he called Sean to get the status of the vehicles. Sean claimed they were on their way on a car carrier trailer marked with SSG Transportation and Shipping. After that he wrote a draft contract to place several soldiers in the local police stations, as well as to provide the weaponry and armor for the SWAT teams. After reviewing it, he added, 'after observation of tactics at Triskelion facility'. Devon then had his guards, issued by TC, take him to city hall for the intercity location and the local police stations.

As he came into a sheriff's office, the front desk attendant jumped out of their seat and ran back, dragging the sheriff to the door. After talking to him for a few minutes Devon knew that Garmaggio was the local authority here. He had the town on lockdown by blackmailing law enforcement. Devon realized this when the sheriff mentioned payment before the words contract left Devon's mouth.

"Sheriff, I'm not an associate of Don Garmaggio."

"Oh, then why are you here, no one crosses him, he leads the—"

"I know. I've met him already and know his friends, but I work for the organization that they are supposed to follow. I can get Garmaggio off your back."

As soon as he finished his sentence, two of the thugs that assailed his office the night before walked in.

"Watch," Devon says, turning around. "You all know Armando and Francois?"

The two men nod their heads and attempt to look tough while sizing up Triskelion forces, while Devon's forces square up.

"Have you seen them recently?" Devon asks. When they nod he continues. "I did that without the help of my elite forces here, you really want to try this?"

They immediately back down and shake their heads.

"Good. Now leave, you will no longer bother these officers of the law, and tell Garmaggio that from here on out, the local authorities are working under my protection. If he attempts to cross that, he'll deal with me and the Cupola. Now go on!"

The mafioso couldn't get out of the sheriff's office fast enough. Devon then turns and faces the sheriff.

"That was very impressive. However, what did you mean by 'under your protection'?"

"Simple, just sign this document allowing several of my men to work alongside your guys with the full weight of the law, and I'll have someone posted here twenty-four/seven to ensure that Garmaggio doesn't mess with you. I already have the police commissioner's signature but because you work through the sheriff's department, and not police, I'll need your signature as well."

"That's it? Just allow your guys to work with ours?"

"Yes, well and a small fee for any criminals we bring in, the fee is to be determined by the type of criminal detained. This is a temporary contract, if you see in paragraph three, line five, it states that you are welcome to a demonstration at our warehouse, and upon your acceptance there, you'll be issued a full-term contract."

"After that demonstration, I don't need any more proof but all right. What exactly are you doing for the commissioner?"

"The same thing, and we are improving the vehicles with armor, as well as supplying their officers and SWAT teams with armor and weapons."

"Ah, well could we work that into this deal as well? This is a dangerous neighborhood with Garmaggio and all."

"Certainly, if you all would like, I could set that up."

They agree and Devon walks out, successful. He now has not only the cooperation of the local authorities but also the approval to act on their behalf, and get money for it.

As he pulls up to the office, Devon sees a Bell V-280 Valor take off with six fully-equipped specialty assassins. As he walks in, he's greeted by TC at the reception desk who, after explaining the qualifications of the team that just left to complete the ten assassination contracts faxed over from Acerbi International, goes to the security operations office, where cameras show views of all deployed forces and the vitals for each as well. OG is in the office opposite talking on the phone in Moroccan, the words for arms and shipment sticking out.

Devon walks into his office and picks up the phone himself and dials the all too familiar number of his friend from high school.

"Hey Xander, it's Dev. How have you been?"

"Good, bub. Been a while since I heard from you, last time was when you got back from that corporate retreat two months ago."

"Oh yeah, sorry. Been busy. What's your home situation like?"

"Not too good man, we're making it but only by the grace of God."

"Yeah, I can understand that, I was like that a while ago. What would you say if I could give you a job guaranteeing you a better situation? The only contention is that you'll need to move to Columbus, OH."

"I'd have to talk to Grace, but I don't think she'd have a problem with it."

"All right, well I'm going up to my ski lodge next week. You all want to join me and we'll discuss it there?"

"Sure bud. See you then. Kids can come, right?"

"Yeah. Also, I'm gonna have a few friends from college there too, we kind of started this thing together."

"All right. It'll be nice to finally meet some of the guys you spoke so highly of. Ah, Grace is calling. See ya bub!"

After hanging up the phone, Devon walks into the warehouse just in time to see the SSG truck pull up with luxury cars, SUVs, and trucks with the SUVs clearly having the upper hand in the vehicle competition. As Devon approaches the truck, he's met by Marcus Fonte, Sean's first capo.

"Don Gregory, it's an honor!"

"Thank you, Fonte, now give me the specs on all these vehicles as you unload them onto the lot. OG, get a couple teams to transport these vehicles to the garage for security protocol enhancements."

Fonte explains that one-third of SUVs aren't SUVs at all but UAVs, Urban Assault Vehicles. They have four bucket seats and the back seats are against the sides of the vehicles with a machine gun station at the back center. There were also Lamborghinis, Bentleys and Porsches in the assortment. After detailing the full specifications from engine type to tailpipe, Devon had the vehicles taken to the garage. As Devon walks into the office, OG meets him at the door.

"Want me to head over to the garage and oversee the armoring process?"

"No, this is an upper level Mafia task and I will oversee it personally, I need you to finish setting up the arms deals. We have a meeting in two weeks and I want to have some jobs in every ring completed by then."

"Of course, sir!"

Devon then grabs TC and heads over to the garage, across the street. As soon as they walked in, they set to work, they had all the vehicles start to be dismantled, tagged, and recorded. Then they met with Vector Hale, a former lead vehicle mechanic for the Green Berets and Delta Force who had worked with private security armoring when off duty. Devon informed him that the vehicles receive the best armoring with minimal depletion of miles per gallon. After that Devon turned to TC.

"How's the contracts coming?"

"All teams went dark about thirty minutes ago, if we don't receive word in thirty minutes, we're to assume failure."

"All right, keep me posted I want to know when the jobs are accomplished so I can get in touch with Don Acerbi's contact and set up a fund transfer. They know to get photo evidence and a token, correct?"

"Yes. Also, I have almost finished pulling the information together for the enforcer and security force training. Is there anything else I need to know that is on my list?"

"Oh. Yes, I need you to start assembling information for a trip to assess security protocols for each family location and to dispense proper security forces," Devon informs him while exiting the garage.

"All right, when does this need to be ready?"

"We start a week after the meeting, so if you have it done within three days after the meeting, we'll be good to go. That's a whole package deal from departure to return."

"Yes, sir. It will be done," TC says, opening the door to the office.

Devon walks into his office and sees that it was three thirty. He must meet Victoria for a doctor's appointment across town at four thirty, so he checks in with OG and learns that several smuggling operations have been organized to be carried out over the next few days. With that information noted, he tells OG to keep him posted and climbs into his Lincoln Navigator, immediately heading across town.

As he pulls up at the doctor's office, TC informs him that they're closely approaching time to hear from the stealth operations teams' deadline for contact and only half have reported in.

"Keep constant communication open. I want to know every detail as it happens."

"Of course, sir, do you want me to accompany you inside?"

"The office, yes, the room no."

Later, when Devon and TC get back in the Navigator to head back to the office, they're contacted, via the satellite phone in the vehicle, by Don Acerbi himself saying that his operative is awaiting Don Gregory at his office. TC then steps on the gas and gets there within a quarter of the time, using their ties in the law enforcement areas to get them a legal escort across town.

Devon walks into the office, heads straight to his loft conference room, where the more confidential meetings take place, and is met by a laughing OG and Francesca Acerbi, the eldest child of Carmine Acerbi, and recently promoted to underboss of the Acerbi family. As Devon walked in, OG's laughter stopped almost abruptly,

"That'll be all Mr. Fiore, Ms Acerbi and I have professional matters to attend to. If you would, could you go and check the law enforcement contracts we've established, make the necessary pickups of arrest and detainment fees?"

"Of course, sir."

As Conner left the room, Francesca rose from her seat. Devon approached her and shook her hand before taking his seat.

"Don Devon Gregory, chief enforcer of the Maretelli syndicate, my name is Francesca Acerbi, daughter of Don Carmine Acerbi of Acerbi International Technologies and Cupola seat member. I've recently taken up the gauntlet of underboss for my father's organization and your name stuck out. My naïve sister contacted you earlier this week about a set of stealth ops the Cupola needed completed, correct?"

"She did, and as of four forty-five, those contracts were completed. I was just about to send the photo evidence to her for verification before fund transfers were initiated. The Gregorian family prides itself on accuracy."

"Well as respectable as that is, that was not within her place to call you to complete those and as such was not able to give you the full parameters of the missions. How did she come across you?"

"I don't know I placed OG, ah sorry, Conner Fiore, the man here a few minutes ago, in charge of setting up those operations. I just received an email, printed the attached files and set my forces to work, selecting the best men for the job."

"They certainly were the right men for the jobs you thought you were getting into, and for that we will compensate you. However, since you weren't properly informed and therefore mishandled the situation, we'll need to cut the pay rate. You'll only be receiving sixty-five percent of the stated amount, and that's because it's our end that caused the issue. Also you need to deal with Fiore, he was flaunting himself around with my sister, which led to her assistance and the problem."

"Yes, madam. Anything else?"

"No. And keep the tokens you took, always take tokens of the first jobs in each ring you're involved with."

With that she got up, and exited the room. Devon soon followed and immediately found OG.

"Never again."

"What? Entertain until you arrive?"

"No, that was fine. I mean never again woo us into getting contracts. That led to us mishandling them and we just got a drastic reduction in pay."

"What do you mean?"

"I mean never again use your talents as a ladies' man to land us contracts because it leads to potential miscommunication. We didn't handle the contracts right because the one who sent them wasn't in charge of that and didn't give us the full details. Which means your ridiculous actions led to botched contracts."

"All right. Noted, but we got a problem closer to home."

"What is it?"

"Don Garmaggio contacted us."

"What does that underrated bigshot want?"

"To meet on neutral territory. Family to family. All capos, the underboss, everyone. Tomorrow midday," OG informs the don blatantly.

"I wonder why. I have a perfect location, but we'll need it scouted before and surrounded by forces," Devon determines.

"All right, where? I'll send our teams to survey and set positions up."

"A condemned skyscraper in upper Manhattan, Roc Security, fifteenth floor conference room. Just tell him the Roc building, he'll know where to go."

"All right. Will do. Sorry about the contract thing."

"It's in the past, just don't let it happen again."

Devon then leaves the building, and heads home to retire for the night with his wife and unborn child.

Chapter 5

The days following the Acerbi meeting were abuzz with everyone making the necessary adjustments and final preparations for the meeting. Conner Fiore was always in and out of the facility, making runs to the docks to retrieve items and teams from his latest operations, TC was overseeing the cataloging and organization of the most recent detachment of equipment and checking the reinforcement process of the vehicles, while Devon was reviewing the latest selection of people chosen to move up in security clearance within the family as well as being the overseer of the personnel on tasks, and double checking contracts to ensure no more slip-ups.

The day after Ms Acerbi left, Devon, TC, Conner, and their eight capos all traveled to the Roc Security building for the Garmaggio meeting. When they arrived, the capos made a diamond formation around their boss, underboss, and chief enforcer while TC and Conner stood side by side in front of Devon. They entered the building and walked up to the landing where the elevators were located, only one elevator was operational to maintain control of the meeting. Conner had three teams patrolling the stair chambers and two teams aligned on the first and fifteenth floors, as well as forces scattered throughout the surrounding buildings. Devon and his associates made their way up to the fifteenth floor conference room and positioned themselves accordingly, the eight capos aligned along the walls. Devon sat at the head of the table with TC on the right and OG on the left. After waiting for almost two hours, they heard the ringing of the elevator, alerting them to the arrival of their guests. Don Cesare Garmaggio walked into the room with an elite guard of three along with his underboss, enforcer and consigliere.

"That's a sparse security detail, Josephs?"

"Well I didn't set this meeting for a strike, although I'm impressed by how well your forces covered this meeting, it certainly shows I made the right call."

"Right call? What's going on here, Howard?"

"It's simple really. But tell me something first, why here?"

"I thought it'd be symbolic, to meet here again."

"Fair enough. I asked for this meeting for one reason. As you know I'm the most powerful, most influential boss on the Commission at this time, earning me the title boss of bosses. Therefore, it only makes sense that I be the one to make this offer."

"Offer?"

"Yes. You see, last night I sent couriers to the other Commission bosses and discussed, well discussed you. You're the first real threat this syndicate has seen since John Gotti was taken down in the nineties. You were bold in staking a claim in the center of my territory, while the other bosses in your syndicate all took fringe claims, on the edge of local Commission boss territory. You've proven you have skill, as such instead of working outside the Commission, we've decided to offer you a place among the Commission, as our overall security coordinator. Every Commission boss enforcer and security detail will report to you. What do you say?"

"I may not be a lot of things to you, but know this, my greatest attribute is loyalty. So, thanks, but no thank you. This meeting is over. Good day, Cesare."

With that Devon walked out on the most powerful mafioso in the country. As his Navigator pulled up to the garage, Vector was loading the last vehicle onto the Chinook helicopter carrying the security equipment to be delivered after the meeting next week. Devon then settled into his office and considered his most recent emails. As a matter of business, all contract recipients are asked to contact him one week after their contract is met. Most reports were good, OG was handling the smuggling affairs to an awesome degree, TC was managing the personnel contracts to a level of exquisite completion and Devon was overseeing all of it while managing the contracts signed with the US military and managing the soldiers placed within the police departments and working in that respect. With all the contracts moving in and out of their office, the next week went by in the blink of an eye. The night before they departed, Cesare Garmaggio called Devon and ceded control of his family to Devon. Devon then set Garmaggio as his acting boss (a puppet boss to stay informed of Commission activities) and limited all contact with him. To the Cupola and Commission, Garmaggio was still in charge, but Devon really held all the cards in his hand.

On Friday, March 27, Devon drove his personal Escalade onto the Chinook chopper and then leads Horrus to the Triskelion Bell V-280 Valor for executive use only. After TC and OG arrive and pile in along with three of their capos, the elite pilot prepared for take-off and everyone strapped up. It wasn't a long lift, but it was a high one.

They landed on the side of a mountain, just two hundred and fifty yards into the woods from where the only road up the mountain ended. One hundred and fifty feet above them sat Devon's ski lodge, which he bought four years into his career with Roc Security. After they land, a couple more choppers come in and three off road trucks and SUVs pull forward out of the tree line.

Devon climbs out of the chopper with TC in tow, and approaches the motorcade, stopping midway. As he descended from the helicopter, the other bosses climbed out of their vehicles and met him in the center of the grove.

"I thought we were meeting at your lodge?" Sean asks as the group gathers.

"We are, but it can't be accessed by road, we'll need to load onto the Chinook which will land us safely there. It is the perfect location for our meetings, inaccessible to unwanted guests," Devon reveals.

"What of our vehicles?" Xavier wonders.

"Devon has a hidden garage, in the cliffside where our security forces and transportation can sit and relax while we discuss business. Shall we continue so we can get out of this chilly air?" TC states.

They all take seats in the choppers that landed with Devon's and are smoothly lifted to the lodge, while their other vehicles were relocated to the specified coordinates Devon gave them. When they landed, they were met by Francois Cartier, Devon's personal property steward, and Xander Sullivan, Devon's hopeful consigliere. As everyone got settled into the lounge, Devon asked for Xander to follow him to the office. Devon wanted to keep his family affairs sequestered from other Mafia discussions, so he had to approach Xander privately. Once they were alone in the office, Devon asked the all-important question:

"Xander, all these people are here tonight to have the first official meeting of the Maretelli syndicate, and the reason you were invited was because I'd like to bring you into the fold as my family's consigliere, or adviser. I'll give you the same deal I gave TC and Conner, full amnesty in any prosecutions that come from our activities. The benefits are that you'll get about two thousand five hundred dollars per week and a full security detail for you and your family. What do you say?" Devon asks, extending his hand.

"I say, let's get down to business." Xander grabs and shakes his friend's hand and rises to his feet.

They exit the office and return to the others just in time for the pre-meeting meal to begin. Tonight's course included Caesar salads, steaks with baked potatoes, steamed broccoli and sweet carrots, and then the meal is finished off with a slice of New York style strawberry cheesecake and a small bowl of banana pudding. It was perhaps the most delightful meal Devon had ever experienced, small talk happening between everyone and delicious food. As the two maids removed the dishes from the table, Antonin stood.

"Well, Devon give my compliments to the staff on a very delightful meal, but I believe it is time we get down to business, so if the gentlemen will follow Devon to the private meeting room, and if the ladies and children would be so kind as to enjoy the evening in the lounge."

With that, everyone begins to disperse, with the men following Devon and the women and children retiring to the lounge. Devon leads the men through the office, where he opens a book sitting on the desk and presses in a code. Once the code is entered, the fireplace recedes into the wall, revealing a stairwell that descends into the depths of the lodge. When they exit at the bottom of the stairwell, they are in a dimly lit conference room with a round table with eleven seats around it and ten stools situated along the wall. Each boss and consigliere took seats at the table while enforcers and underbosses took their places on stools behind their boss. The extra seat was filled by Dominic Oberti, the Cupola liaison for their syndicate.

"Gentlemen, on behalf of the Cupola, under the leadership of the *capo di tutti i capi*, I'm happy to oversee this initial meeting of the Maretelli syndicate and I need to ask you all how you will recognize each other, or members of the families within your syndicate. So, we need to cement your commitments to each other and then when you all return to your bases of operation administer a similar commitment to your soldiers. So, what shall it be?" he began.

"I believe that it needs to be something deeply vested in each of us: a blood oath. My idea is that we each have a pint of blood taken, we mix it together and each boss chooses something small like a ring or necklace. Then we each take a small portion of the combined plasma and embed it into that thing to be worn by those in this room. The bosses could all have the same small brand, and the family members each have a visible tattoo with similar attributes of the brand the bosses have, but with the main symbol of their tattoo being chosen by their boss," Devon offers up.

"That could work, if it's done right," Dominic contests.

So, a vote was taken and everyone agreed to Devon's plan. With Antonin having a background in the medical field before politics, he was delegated to draw the blood. When all the blood was drawn and combined in an urn, items were brought forward, selected by each boss: rings, necklaces, bangles, belt buckles, and ear piercings. Then an argument ensues to determine the brand. Antonin says a horse, Xavier wants a lion and Sean wants snakes, of course, considering his call-sign, that's no surprise. After much discussion, Devon silences them all.

"Gentlemen, let's think rationally. You are all considering things important to yourselves. However, the brand is what unites all the bosses at this table, so it should be something we share. What about this? A shield with a goblet on it, with two swords crossed beneath it, above it a banner reading '*en vino, veritas*'. The tattoos can differ in their main symbol, instead of a goblet, Sean can have a snake, Xavier can have a lion, so on and so forth."

"Fair enough for me," Antonin says.

"Devon, you have a real talent with compromise. Has anyone ever talked to you about taking the official title of Maretelli consigliere, the chief adviser of the family?" Dominic mentions.

At that suggestion, votes are taken and Devon is made the consigliere of the family and his idea was adopted as the symbol system they'd use. Then they moved on to official business, informing the group on each of their individual successes. Antonin went first being the boss. He took office as governor of Arizona and from that office was able to institute one of Devon's capos as adjutant general, appoint one of Xavier's capos to the Economic Security Advisory Council, place one of Sean's family on the Board of Executive Clemency, and ensure Aaron's capo was put on the Arizona Commerce Authority board of directors.

With his underboss in the position of acting boss, he turns to him and asks for the update on his assigned rings. He then reported that all rings were operational and functioning smoothly with a gross income of one point three million dollars, which meant that each boss would receive Two hundred thousand dollars from his family alone. Next, following the chain of superiority, Devon gave his report. Devon had come in to the meeting with a total gross income for his family of three point five million dollars, raising everyone's take-away sum by six hundred thousand dollars. He was about to give Sean his chance to update when TC whispered something about Garmaggio in his ear. Devon shook his head, not wanting to reveal his ace in the hole.

"That's all to report now, Sean?"

Sean had made significant gains as well, bringing in nearly two million dollars. Aaron brought in two point three million dollars and Xavier brought in three point two million dollars. In the end each person left with just over two million dollars and they had a Mafia account balance of two million dollars as well. Dominic took the Cupola cut of two hundred and fifty thousand dollars from the Mafia account leaving them with one point seven five million dollars for Mafia expenses. After they finished reviewing numbers and separating money, Devon led the bosses out to the balcony to distribute the vehicles, while TC took the enforcers to the library for training.

"Gentlemen, I present to you, your vehicle convoys. Each family has a specific type of vehicle that corresponds with their location. Sean, Xavier and I all have luxury cars in our family sets because we live in high-end areas of the nation. Aaron has off-road vehicles and Antonin has semi-luxury vehicles. Each family convoy includes two to six security vehicles, Chevy Suburbans enhanced the same as the delegated vehicles except with more weapons caches. Xavier's family will get Lexus vehicles, Antonin will get Rolls Royce Phantoms, Sean will get Mercedes Benz vehicles, Aaron will have Land Rovers, and I will get Cadillacs. We've customized each vehicle with the highest-grade armoring worldwide, which is classified intel only available to myself and the armoring team. Also, all your drivers have been trained in emergency driving, ensuring your maximum safety. All other vehicles you need will be requisitioned through Sean, transported to me for security protocols and then sent your way. Now I believe our security and wives are waiting for us in the parlor."

After all business had been taken care of, everyone spent the remainder of the evening enjoying one another's company. The ladies talked around the fireplace, the men enjoyed their drinks and played billiards while any kids that were brought enjoyed movies in the private theater.

Upon returning to their home the following day, Victoria painted in her art studio while Devon stayed confined to his office, planning the first security check-up trip as well as coordinating envoys for his expansion into the national law enforcement agencies. They then ordered in dinner and just relaxed, and spent time with one another.

Chapter 6

The next Monday, Devon and TC began pulling documents and setting things up for the trip to Washington DC to meet the national security agencies representatives. They selected only the best of the elite squadrons to accompany them. After selecting the teams and going through the proper representation in the setting they were going to be in, everyone loaded into the Suburbans, and Devon and TC placed the Escalade in the choppers and boarded the stealth one. Once seated, Devon gave the go ahead for lift off.

When they landed at Andrews Air Force Base, they were met by an attaché of Special Forces that escorted them to the Pentagon. Instead of going from office to office, Devon had asked for an audience with the major leaders of the national security community. This includes the directors of the FBI, CIA, NSA, US marshals, Department of Defense and all its sub-departments, and the joint chiefs of staff. The meeting was to be held at the Pentagon, the home of the Department of Defense and Devon agreed to such terms if he could bring a contingency of his own forces. As they entered the

Pentagon, Devon and TC led two of the ten teams they brought into the facility. Upon their entrance into the facility, everyone moved out of their way while one of the security officers escorted them to the conference area to set up for the presentation.

"I will alert the secretary and his guests that you've arrived."

"Good. Request that I will be ready in fifteen minutes at the latest."

"Of course."

After the officer had closed the door Devon turned to TC. TC then reached into his pocket and pulled a device out, placing it along the bottom lip of central desk of the conference room.

"Now that we're not being heard, everyone be ready. Watch for my signal and then move as we coordinated at headquarters," Devon says just as the device falls from the desk. TC picks it up and slips it in his pocket.

"So just position yourself here, holding the prototype like so."

Devon steps away from the officer, and stands before the desk, with TC flanking his right side as the door opens and a Secret Service agent walks in, followed by a barrage of national security leaders, including the commander in chief of the United States military.

Devon then directs TC to begin the pseudo demonstration they put together to have their men positioned accordingly, TC then turns to face the teams and coordinates their movements. Afterward he turns to face the president. Devon closes his eyes and slowly nods, for a second a light in each corner of the room flickers.

Devon looks up and slowly smiles.

"Mr. President, members of the National Security Council, and other assembled parties. I'm sorry the secretary had to get you all in here for that measly demonstration, but all is not lost. You see, for the past week my forces have infiltrated the Pentagon security force and my officers within these walls just gave me direct control of all security in this building. They've shut off the recording equipment both visual and audio so the only record you have of my demonstration is the demonstration. And the Secret Service can't do anything for two reasons. One Our contract that allowed me entry says no weapons will be brought into the facility by either party. The demonstration weapons are all plastic mock-ups so they fit that criteria. Two. My men are positioned in just the right areas to disarm those forces in less than five seconds if need be. So, let's have a rational discussion about transferring some authority, shall we? Here's my proposition, Mr. President, you give me control of thirty-five percent of all military forces under your command, and direct all the others in this room to do the same with their forces both military, intelligence, and otherwise, and we all walk away happy."

"Are you mad?" the secretary of defense cries out.

"No. I'm former Colonel Devon Jacob Gregory of Delta Force. One of the highest decorated commanders that unit has ever had. I redeveloped the training process for you too before retiring. This is my former XO and successor, former Colonel Travis Carson Richards. We now run the Triskelion Security Corporation."

"So, you're just insane?" Secretary of Defense Nicholas Brazien says.

"No, he's completely sensible, Mr Secretary, sir!" Vice Chairman Donahue speaks up.

"And just how do you know that Vice Chairman?"

"Because he watched as I took command of sixty-five percent of the US Special Forces about two months ago."

"Excuse me! He what?" the secretary shouts.

"You heard him. Colonel Gregory has been in control of some portion of our forces, up to sixty-five percent of which he has command of. So, any missions they've successfully completed are due to his credit. I've never seen men so dedicated, passionate, and powerful, as the ones he's taken under his command."

"So, if he has control of them, how are we still using them?" the president asks as if not hearing any of the past couple minutes of insults across the room.

"I'll answer that Mr Chairman, thank you though, for pointing that out. You are using them through a contract with my firm. I have ultimate control over the forces you give me, and ninety-five percent of those forces stay attached to your command if I have no other need for them. Over the course of weeks, I take parts of them and retrain them through our specially designed program that enhances their abilities. You can use them at your discretion if I get whichever ones I need when necessary.

You all can either agree to this contract, which former Colonel Richards is passing out, or I make a call and pull all sixty-five percent of Special Forces off the grid and the US covert operations crumble around you as the world runs into chaos. What do you say?"

"Before you agree, sir, what's the economic means? You're a business man now Colonel Gregory. What's the catch?" the secretary of the treasury asks.

"The four hundred and fifty billion dollars portioned for the operations of these forces. However, for the first terms of this contract instead of giving me the money, you use it to pay off the national debt. Once that's been paid down to a sizeable sum of about two point five trillion, then you all pay me that sum, forty percent of which I will reinvest in keeping the debt down. How's that sound? That's ten years you all won't have to pay me and I'll still fulfill my obligations of the agreement. This agreement has a twenty-year lifespan, and supersedes political terms, so no matter the change in politics over the next score, this contract will remain."

"DEAL!" the president exclaims. "I can't deal with any more bickering about debt. At least this is a workable plan, right Mr Secretary?"

"Of course, sir," the secretary of the treasury responds timidly.

"Mr. President, I would strongly advise against this, to give over control of any portion of our intelligence and law enforcement agencies to the private sector would be madness and I won't agree to it," the secretary of defense challenges.

"Secretary Brazien, this is not a suggestion any more. I've made my decision, and I'm ordering you as your commander in chief to sign this agreement, or face dismissal and I'll find someone who will follow my commands," the president proclaims sternly.

"Yes, commander, but I want it on record that I'm against this."

"It will be noted in our records. Thank you, Mr. President and everyone. I will send escorts to acquire my first section of associates within the next few weeks. Good Day!" Devon states, walking out of the facility, which then receives full control of its security database.

Devon and TC then climb into the Escalade with Horrus and begin the drive to Orlando, Xavier's base of operations, with the small contingency that he requested as his enforcer brigade.

Chapter 7

Upon arriving in Orlando they went to the office and apartment space Triskelion had recently acquired, which was right across from The Barrel, Xavier's first club. The office was to become the base of operations of his enforcer brigade, led by Cole Garvey, Xavier's chief enforcer, who met them at the office with Xavier.

"Bullet, how are things?" They grip each other.

"Well, business the past couple of weeks has been awesome, but last night we had a major security screw up with the temporary guys I had on hand."

"We can't have any of that. But that's why I'm here. Let's discuss things, yes?"

"Of course." Xavier motions to the high back office chair behind the desk.

Devon takes a seat, while TC stands at his right side, opposite Xavier and Cole in the same fashion. TC then places a briefcase on the left end of the desk, and opens it. He then removes a contract and pulls a small mahogany box from one of the pockets in the case. He opens the box and pulls out its contents, revealing a magnificent Imperial style mahogany fountain pen with a gold clip. Xavier can't help but stare.

"You like? It's a gift from Don Acerbi for taking out the highest mark on his black list, a small-time rival boss that evaded his personal bounty hunters."

"It's wonderful. I wish I had one to even compare."

"You're in luck. I received a couple similar ones in black and titanium finish. I was going to let you sign with it and tell you to keep it then, but here you are." TC fetches a box like the first, but black, and hands it to Devon, who then opens it and extends it to Xavier.

"Now to official business. I have requisitioned for your use fifteen security officers, as your businesses grow we will send more to accommodate your needs. Also, we will be sending a logistics team to oversee the video surveillance as well as a resident close combat specialist. Any other specialist you need, just contact myself, TC, or our office to request them and we will discharge them to the best of our availability. Now if you'll sign on the dotted line at the bottom of this page, you'll be made the CO of the team, with Cole acting CO, as your XO while you handle all other matters. For all intents and purposes, you are in command of all the men given herein. However, at any time I find necessary, I retain the right to pull them from duty if I see fit, being the chief executive officer of Triskelion Security, the firm they're employed through, working on behalf of the Roc Security Company," Devon explains, pushing the contract to Xavier's side of the desk.

"Very well," Xavier says, signing the agreement.

TC then snaps a picture of the document.

"The agreement is now being sent to an international server file, inaccessible unless certain codes are entered on three separate databases. A copy is simultaneously being printed in your office at the club, at home, at my house, and here. Being the facilitator of the contract, the original will be kept with me for my office records."

"With business being completed, would you like to adjourn to The Barrel for a couple of celebratory drinks?"

"I see no reason why not. TC, will you walk Cole through the command protocol, show him the best placements for these officers, and discharge them to his command, then come meet us at the bar?"

"Of course, sir."

Devon and Xavier then walk to the bar, which was still preparing to open for the night, where Devon orders a scotch and Xavier gets a gin and tonic, to which the head bartender replies, "Yes boss!"

After getting their drinks Devon and Xavier have a pleasant conversation and when TC arrives, Xavier walks the pair around and Devon and TC point out the best points for security cameras and such. Once they tallied the total security package needed to cover the facility, TC texted OG the details, so he could start preparing the shipments. Then they all sat down as Cole joined them, having positioned the officers, and the bar opened. They had just taken seats at one of the booths when Devon received a call. He got up and went outside, followed by TC.

"Hello?"

"Devon, I just got off the phone with the asset (the term used for Garmaggio over all telecommunication in the family), he's flipping out about something..." OG begins.

Just then, about ten police cruisers flew by, behind black SUVs with federal plates, headed into Commission territory, followed by a couple of helicopters and three SWAT trucks. Devon then knew what was going on.

"I told him that you'd get back to him at your earliest convenience," Fiore finishes.

"Thank you for informing me, call them and patch me to them, then get off the line Conner."

"Yes, sir." Then there are a few taps and the line opens back up.

"Howard, using his US record name to cover their conversation, what's going on?"

"Devon, there's a major crash happening on the network. I'm worried our stocks may be lost," Garmaggio states in the code they'd created which translates as, 'The feds, state and local agencies are coordinating a mass arrest of all Commission related families and businesses and he's worried that his subordinate families and businesses will be taken'.

"Howard, don't worry. I re-evaluated your stock options and reinvested. Your savings will be fine," Devon replies, informing him that since Devon took charge, he had considered each family and cover business and given them semi-legitimate fronts, like Sean and Xavier had done with their businesses and families. Therefore, they'd be fine.

"Very well. I trust you, Devon, don't let me down."

"Was that a threat Mr. Josephs, because our agreement states no threats or harmful action will be brought against me as long as I work in the best interest of the whole, which I am. This is good for us."

"How so?" Garmaggio wonders.

"The other brokers will come to you to see how you stayed afloat at which point you could tell them to consider a partner firm of mine [cover to not connect Garmaggio with Gregory] and that it will get them back into the market [allow them to replace their ineffective security detail with Devon's forces unbeknownst to them] increasing your trade ability [raise Devon and Garmaggio influence on Commission issues]."

"I see. Thank you!"

With that Devon closed the line and went back inside. Upon approaching Xavier, he asked to return to business for situations that had just occurred needed to be discussed.

"Of course, dear friend, it's in the storage closet for safe keeping," Xavier says.

They make their way through the crowded bar and walk into a door labeled 'AUTHORIZED PERSONNEL ONLY', and on the other end of the wall, a similar door reading, 'VIP CUSTOMERS ONLY, PLEASE HAVE BADGES READY', guarded by two of the Green Beret forces they brought.

On the other side of the door is a strip club, with scantily clad women dancing on poles set on a stage extending in a U-shape around the whole room. Hanging around the room were cages with poles running through their center and dancing in the cages were completely bare women. Across the two side walls were privacy booths, and at the back were showcase rooms, flanked by two doors marked 'PRIVATE ROOMS. PLEASE RESERVE AT DESK!'

"Office?" Devon mouths over the booming music, which couldn't be discernibly heard from the other side of the bar, but still created a faint booming sound through the complex.

Xavier points up at the large platform above them and then leads them to a small closet where a spiral staircase was hidden. They exit into an inverted trapezoidal room where the two slanted edges are one-way mirrors. In the back of the room was situated a desk in front of a fireplace, flanked by bookcases. The center of the room was dominated by a conference table and along the wall nearest their entrance was a couch on the other side of which was another door, leading to a spiral staircase to reach the bar, Devon assumed. Sitting between the couch and conference table sat a simple glass top desk, with a computer on top. Behind the desk, on the conference table side, typing on the computer was Celina Jones, Bullet's 'Doll face' wife, and apparently, secretary.

"Celina, good to see you again. Bullet I like this set-up, you can view both the legit and illicit side of your operation." Devon spoke with confidence, hoping that Xavier had placed the debugging device beneath the conference table to scramble or disable any intercepting technology.

"Thank you. What happened that caused us to retire to my office?"

"Before I speak, I must have your sole word that we're in pact together. From here I hit Fort Wayne, where Sean is and will inform him as well, hopefully pulling him into this pact."

"Yeah, totally. What's up?"

"*En vino veritas, Sacrum Vinculum*?"

"*Sacrum Vinculum*!" Xavier responds, crossing his forearm with Devon's, referring to their sacred pact of brotherhood in life unto death.

"Cesare Garmaggio ceded power of his entire network to me the night before the first meeting."

"What, so we already have power in the Commission?"

"No, I already have a spy in the Commission. We have a plan that I'm willing to let you and Sean in on, if you all keep this on the down-low. I don't want to expose my whole hand just yet."

"What would I get out of it?"

"Control of all Mafia-run clubs nationwide when we oust the Commission from power for the Cupola."

"How are you going to get the Cupola to agree?"

"Let me handle the specifics, you in?"

"HYB! So, what's this incident?"

"The federal and state governments just began a massive execution of what they call Operation Mike Tango Delta, a nationwide arrest of all Mafia affiliated businesses and persons. An operation that, as of seventy-two-hours ago, I became a part of."

"What, won't that crush our plan?"

"Actually, it will help both plans for us. One the Mafia will need to expand boundaries, bringing all of us into the loop, helping the Cupola plan. Second, they'll blame their security/enforcers, which will allow Garmaggio, the only boss not losing anything, to get them to sign up for my forces through a proxy agency, thus helping my plan."

"That's awesomely terrifying."

"Yeah. Also, if you have any major adversaries that you think will be a problem, just contact me and I'll handle it personally. Your forces have already been told to do so as well. *Sacrum Vinculum*?" Devon informs him.

"*Sacrum Vinculum*!" Xavier replies, repeating their movement from before.

"I will be staying above the office for a few days to ensure my officers are well acquainted before departing for Sean's office in Fort Wayne."

"All right. Well tomorrow, why don't you and TC join Celina and I for dinner at LT Steak and Seafood, I can get us a private table?"

"Certainly, but later, you'll have to invite me to Club Twenty-one, and we'll have a wonderful dinner in the hidden wine cellar from the prohibition days. Deal?"

"If you get me that place, then HYB!"

With that they adjourned to an evening of fun in the bar, much to Xavier's dismay.

The next day Devon oversaw the arrival and installation of the security monitoring station and re-evaluated the positions of the security personnel around the premises of the club. Once approved, Devon stocked the backroom of the office with weapons and vests, as well as set up the database for covert communication between the family. After that was done he retired to prepare for dinner with Xavier and Celina. The days following the dinner went by monotonously, Devon ensured that each security professional was outfitted correctly before and after their shift and that their demeanor was stern yet approachable. After ensuring that this outpost of his family was sufficiently equipped and trained, he used a variety of security measures to secure access to the basement facility of the Triskelion office, where Cole and Bullet were to communicate with the rest of the syndicate. Then climbed into his Escalade and drove to an airfield to fly to Indiana.

They returned to the office almost a month later, having set up the enforcement offices for all the bosses in their syndicate as well as placing some new ones in central areas of the Garmaggio family influence. As Devon walked into the headquarters, he called Conner and the lead capos to the conference room for a brief. Then called Garmaggio and placed him on the intercom of the room.

"Gentlemen. We are officially the largest security corporation in the US, as well as the most powerful family in the nation. I have secured us thirty-five percent of the

US bureaucracy intelligence, law enforcement, and military agencies to add to our sixty-five percent of Special Forces. Having just set up offices throughout the continental US, I need to be brought up to date on all operations of all departments under my charge. OG, what's the status of the black market operations?"

"While you were gone, we executed fifteen orders with five nations, two private armies, and one very ambitious monarch, all following our guidelines to not be informed of usage. Another four orders were shipped as you pulled in, and two other shipments are being prepped and secured for loading. Our estimated income by the fifteenth is five point nine million dollars."

"Very good. TC you've been keeping up with all blacklist enterprises while we've travelled, yes?"

"Yes, sir, and throughout our travels, forty-five marks have been met, thirty have been returned on, fifteen trades are commencing as we speak. Ten more teams are surveying their targets, five are in transit to begin and three are getting their supplies together for take-off. Our anticipated bring in is around six point seven million dollars, excluding any gifts for services rendered."

"Garmaggio, just give me your numbers."

"Twenty-five point seven million dollars from all industries for the last month."

"Well we're certainly raking it in. Garmaggio, we will need a larger space to operate out of."

"I anticipated that, and have recently acquired a facility you might have an interest in. The Old Roc Security office building?"

"That'd be perfect, we'd just have to do minor aesthetical changes since it was a security office before. OG, TC and I will discuss the details of the move later. Garmaggio, have all your forces meet there in couple weeks to receive new uniforms and protocols."

"Yes, sir."

The next day Devon has TC pass the new office on the way to the docks, there were men already there putting up new signs and repairing the old building. They pull up to the docks and meet with OG.

"A few of our shipments were lost."

"What?" Devon responds.

"According to the admiral of section three, who oversees all ships headed below the Mediterranean across the Atlantic, we lost five crates when the ship headed for Morocco ran straight into the path of a tropical storm."

"Sir, we have a couple more issues as well. I just received word from convoy five, that all but one member of their detail was caught trailing the target with deadly weapons nearby," TC adds.

"All right, let's slow down. Conner prepare another set of shipments for the Morocco deal, have them airlifted through the Mediterranean. TC, have convoy five's remaining asset pull back and send a team to back him, then when we get back to the office ask for an extension on the contract, explaining that due to company complications if they grant the extension we'll take twenty-three percent less than the contracted rate. Now get me back home so I can figure out more secure paths for us to use in the future."

After returning home, Devon spends the rest of the day sequestered in the office recalibrating company policy. Once he was happy with the arrangements, he emailed them to OG and TC, before retiring to a night of bliss with Victoria.

The weeks following, all business was going about as if no setbacks had occurred. Devon stopped by the old facility to pick up the last of his materials for the new offices. The final decision was that the most trusted lieutenants under TC and OG would take over running the operations of the small firm using it as a waypoint for the fringe network to secure the borders of the now growing Gregorian territory. Two similar firms would be started at undisclosed locations around the territory's borders for security purposes, ran by the other lieutenants. With a massive increase in the size of the corporation, Devon incorporated the company. All members of all families of the Maretelli syndicate would compose the shareholders' congress, the board of directors would be the other family heads as well as Devon, TC, OG, and Garmaggio. Devon being chief executive officer, obviously, TC being the chief security officer, OG taking the role of chief communications officer, and Garmaggio being the chief strategy officer. The other bosses filled the other roles essential to functionality.

With that being determined, Devon places the last box of materials on his desk, sits in his luxurious new leather office chair and looks out at the city expanse bustling with activity beneath him. Being the offices of his former employer, he knew all the secret passages and such that were hidden within the structure. And he told TC, and just TC, about them so that he could be aware of the main security features of the building, which included, a helicopter pad atop the building, an elevator with its own generator, a subterranean vehicle depot, and a private canal leading to the harbor. Devon used part of his recent income to supply vehicles in the depot and dock of the canal. Including two tankers full of gasoline, an armored truck, and an air-conditioned truck with enough food to last six months on the road.

Upon returning to his new office, Devon makes a few calls and lines up a couple meetings with international bosses in his industries coming into town in the next couple of weeks. Then he receives the meeting information from now Governor Maretelli. When noted, he called TC, OG and Xander into his office.

"Mr. Richards, is the door secure?" Devon asks, seeing if the transmission scramblers are active yet? To which TC nods.

"Very well. I have set up an international meeting of all bosses in our area, outside Cupola influence. We've also obtained the time and date of the next meeting, once again on our property."

"Sir we can use that to our advantage," Conner professes.

"I realize that, Conner, thank you. We need to prepare for the arrival of the international representatives, I doubt all these bosses will come themselves."

The phone rings.

"Hello? Devon, it's Antonin, Aaron's under scrutiny by the local crews, and my office is as well."

"I'll see what I can do my friend," Devon replies hanging the phone up. "TC get me Garmaggio now, if anyone asks, he's an investor. Antonin and Aaron are under scrutiny, which means soon Snakes, Bullet, and I will be too. Time to prepare for revealing our hand."

Chapter 8

The next week, Devon was standing in his private security chamber, accessible via the hidden elevator in his office, when his ear vibrated, signaling that he had a business matter to attend to. He was using the chamber primarily for surveillance on his Commission operation, but gave TC permission to use it for general family matters, and therefore handed it off to his enforcer's staff while he resigned to his office.

"What's going on?"

"The representatives from the international family circuit are here and being placed in various offices until you give the order to gather them," Victoria, who chose to fill in for his secretary, says waiting for him by his office door.

"Thank you, dear. Please inform Cesare of these developments and tell him to arrive at his earliest convenience. Once he arrives, retrieve me from my meeting with OG and Xander," Devon answers.

"Yes, sir. Also, you've got a lot of calls from an unknown international number. Would you like me to keep redirecting them or would you like to take one of the calls?"

"Next time one of those calls come through just let me know and I'll take it," Devon says, knowing it had something to do with the move he'd made on the international underworld.

"All right. I'll go gather the last assignment debriefs and department reports."

"Thank you," Devon responds, stopping at the entrance to his office, he straightens his suit, fixes his hair, and opens the doors.

He smiles faintly as he enters the room and links his meeting with Xavier and Sean, who are having similar meetings in their slightly upgraded facilities as well.

"So, it's been a month and a half since the arrests took place. On our end here, thanks to the help of Mr. Callehann and the Phoenix Security Corporation, we've received and accepted requests for seventy-five Mafia leaders within the US, including the Chicago Outfit and the Commission, and have acquired bases of operation in all major operational areas. We have an anticipated bring in of about one hundred and sixty-eight point three million dollars. We are meeting with international heads of our industry as soon as our asset arrives. How are things looking for you all?"

"Well, like your situation, Devon, following the big takedown, a lot of our competition was eliminated for a small increment of time. In that time, my family took advantage of the opportunity and acquired clubs and casinos across the continental US. Expanding our area of influence exponentially. We anticipate receiving ninety-five point seven million dollars this month alone from all ventures," Xavier informs the trio.

"We've done the same here in the Midwest too. The arrests freed up the roadways and left a lot of companies without trucks, for a minute, so my team and I flew in and took over those trucking contracts. We face the challenge of keeping those deals, however, because I've started to receive pressure from an unknown source claiming to know of my connections with the dark underbelly of society. Due to those issues, I'm seeing a bring in of just barely fifty-seven point one million dollars," Sean explains.

"All right, Sean don't worry, I'll have my guys investigate this source and we'll handle it. We all did the right thing though by taking advantage of this opportunity. We need to maintain those positions. Also, when it comes time to report quarterly funding, withhold around a third of what you actually brought in."

As he was about to continue the meeting, Victoria called him on his earpiece to inform him that they were receiving a call from the anonymous number again. Devon excused himself from the meeting, allowing Xander and OG to convey the rest of his ideas and thoughts. He then made his way to his office and picked up the receiver.

"Hello, this is Dr Devon Gregory, CEO and President of Triskelion Security. How may I help you?"

"Don Gregory, you need to relinquish the holdings you've recently established nationwide or face the consequences of challenging the Odessa. We do, however, thank you for getting rid of our Commission problem." Immediately when Devon heard Don, he pressed a red button on the phone.

"You have no idea who you are crossing, I'm an official delegation of the Cupola, which if I know underworld vernacular, is a partner organization to the Bratva. Do not threaten me for you have no idea the real power I hold. Good day!" Devon responds by hanging up the phone.

Devon leaves his office and is informed that Garmaggio was entering the building. He left his office at the precise moment to intercept him at the elevator bay. As he passed the bay, he was joined by Garmaggio who was escorted by his entourage.

"Don, where are your advisers? And why is it so relaxed in this building? We have some of the most important bosses, or liaisons of such in the building and yet it seems as if there are no additional units walking the halls or guarding the room. If I were you…"

"But you're not. And for your information, we've pulled in ten extra teams on standby in the building. The reason we've not had them out and about the facility is because we are trying to avoid drawing extra attention to ourselves. We are trying to minimize the attention to maintain the legality of the business. Regardless, you are not in charge of the operation, I am. You are an adviser and lower level boss within my ranks."

"Yes, sir, sorry I just didn't know."

"It's not your job to know, it's mine. Whatever relevant information I believe you need I would have sent to you. I will let it pass this time, but next time you question my leadership, I'll give you the same special treatment I gave your enforcers a couple years ago.."

"Understood," Garmaggio concedes.

As they finished their argument, they arrived at the shareholders' conference room, where they set up a conference table that was triple the length and double the width, along with thirty executive office chairs. As they enter, they are met by Devon's other advisers, who are situated at the front of the room, in the center of the conference table. Devon then tells Garmaggio to organize himself and his advisers to take up positions at the other end of the table, the visiting bosses and advisers will situate themselves between the two groups. After Garmaggio and Devon got in the room and got settled, Devon tapped his earpiece and said, "Teams Alpha, Bravo, and Delta begin escorting the visiting bosses to the SCR."

After twenty minutes, the room slowly filled with bosses and advisers, and obviously feuds slowly began to emerge as rival units assembled in the room. Luckily, there were four or five teams positioned throughout the room as the entry processional occurred to ensure that things were peaceful until the meeting commenced.

As the last of the representatives filed in and TC asked them to be seated, Devon got himself a glass of whiskey. Then he started the meeting.

"Ladies and gentlemen, bosses and representatives, welcome to Triskelion Security Corporation. My name is Devon Gregory, consigliere of the Maretelli family, and leader of the Gregorian family. I am a representative of the Cupola and have members within the Commission families. The reason you are all here is to have the opportunity to gain the advantage of my forces. I can recondition your security and enforcement to become the best it can be. My entire staff here at Triskelion is within my family, and most are specialists in their field. All field teams are former Special Forces and most of their support are former intelligence bureau operatives. I myself am a former commander of Delta Force as is my chief enforcer, and my underboss is a former commander of the Green Berets. So, we are extremely overqualified to handle any concerns you face," Devon begins.

"Yes, thank you, Don Gregory. Hello everyone, I'm TC Richards, chief security officer for Triskelion. I also oversee all affairs demanding intervention by security forces for all Triskelion clients. Within the past twelve months Triskelion has handled one thousand, five hundred and eighty-seven knock offs, and are currently active in fifteen countries on private contracts outside underworld business affairs."

"We also have the top armaments on the market, and make sure our men are fully equipped with the latest innovations in security. My name is Conner Fiore, I'm the chief communications officer for Triskelion, and oversee trade, of all divisions, for the corporation. We have outstanding contracts with five of the nations seated on the UN Security Council, and have successfully sold fifty-seven point eight million crates of equipment within the last year," OG pipes in.

"So, bosses and liaisons, as you've heard we've got the American market cornered in every aspect we have interests in, and while my associates in the nightclub and shipping arenas are otherwise preoccupied today, they've made leaps and bounds toward the top of their districts as well. Any questions for my associates or myself?"

"Yes, you say you are working with Cupola authority, but if that is true, wouldn't you be reined in on all these activities by the Commission seats?"

"No," Garmaggio says, rising from his chair for the first time. "I have already taken Don Gregory under my wing, but because of the corporation he's created, he's acting as my front man for all legitimate interests while I run the show for the Commission, so Devon has full Commission support for his activities."

"Sorry Cesare, I didn't realize you had interests in this, honestly I didn't even know you were there."

"Perfectly understandable, but nonetheless, your concern is now voided."

"Very well."

"If that is all, my associates and I have other obligations to attend to, TC will remain in the room until you're all dismissed and can answer any further questions. If you all want to requisition the use of our corporation, just rise from your seat and our agents will escort you back to your private lounges, where the proper paperwork will be awaiting your arrival. Once done, just step out of the lounge and give it to an officer, on your way out. Thank you again, gentlemen."

Devon rose from his seat and walked out followed shortly by OG and Garmaggio. Upon returning to his office, he asks Victoria to bring Xander to the office. Devon poured himself another glass of whiskey, having left his half-empty one in the shareholders' conference room. He then sits in an armchair on the opposite side of the fireplace in his office, and stares into the flames while sipping his whiskey.

Devon was so entranced with the flames, he didn't even notice Xander had arrived until his adviser was slipping by him to sit in the armchair across from him.

"What am I doing bub?"

"You're doing what you must without compromising yourself."

"I mean am I doing the right thing as a father to Nicholas?"

"That's ultimately up to you and Victoria, man. I can't make that call. But for my two cents, with how you're doing it, I think it's going well."

"Yeah but I have lost so much time with them already. I mean I missed his birth and so many of those early memories by staying away to keep them safe. And it's so dangerous , and unnerving, even though there are a ton of things he can learn in this life."

"Then give it up until he's able to be trained."

"The company's still not on its feet yet though, and who would I place in charge of this life?"

"Isn't that what OG, TC, and I are for. To help in the running?"

"All right. After our guests leave, set up a meeting with everyone, after the quarterly family update."

Chapter 9

Devon arrived at the lodge, a week prior to the meeting, with Nicholas, Victoria and Horrus and co. Xander and Francois were there too, of course, being the stewards. Everyone else was scheduled to arrive in a couple days. Devon just needed to escape the fuss of the city and asked Xander to help prepare the property. Xander and his family lived in the pool house, but had free access to everything on the property. Devon and Xander were preparing things for the movers, who were coming the next month to bring the Gregorys' personal effects into the home.

The plan was that after the meeting, Devon will cede power to one of his three associates in the Mafia world, and operate Triskelion's legitimate business interests from the lodge. Luckily this will keep Devon in the loop on all activity with the family, while keeping the front that he is out of life. Basically, he'd be making TC or OG his proxy leader.

He knew that it was risky since they're still considered new in the underworld and just taken on contracts with most of the international circuit. This would be received one of two ways by the other families, the preferred outcome is respect for his decision and the upholding of his wishes. The other outcome is retaliation, either removing him from the Maretelli family or taking him out altogether. Devon was prepared for either result.

That evening, Devon and Xander were meeting in Devon's office, while Victoria was with Xander's family in the pool house, when Devon's proximity alert security alarm went off. He pulled up the cameras and picked up three MI-24 helicopters converging on his landing pad.

"Crocodiles, Xander take most of my guards and protect our wives and children. Horrus and his team along with two guards will be plenty for me to intercept whoever this is," Devon states, knowing none of his friends would arrive this early without warning.

Xander left immediately, while Devon pressed a button on his phone and one of the walls opened to reveal an armory, which Devon accessed, grabbing a Desert Eagle pistol and a Ka-bar knife. As soon as the walls retracted back to their position, the electricity was cut off. Devon closed his eyes and listened carefully until he heard the faint creak of the floorboards. Suddenly, the doors fly open and three men walk through, all in heavy fur coats. The man in the center, the roughest of the three, raised a sawn-off shotgun, pointing it at Devon. In response, Devon sits down and throws his feet up on the desk.

"Don Gregory, you have crossed the Odessa. The Pahkan has issued a declaration of dishonor on you and you are therefore sentenced to die at my hands!"

"That's funny Comrade—"

"Korsch, Dmitri Korsch. And why's your death funny?"

"Dmitri. This is funny because I know that I won't be dying today, or soon, especially by your hands."

"The Pahkan has issued your death."

"When? I just talked to the Pahkan a couple days ago, and if my understanding of the Bratva is correct, you must be one of the spies. Which means you serve the Pahkan directly. So, in about forty-five seconds this phone will ring, I will answer it and then hand it over to you. After said conversation, you will proceed to put your guns down and fly out of here."

"Ha! I doubt that any of that—"

Ring, ring, ring.

Devon reaches for the receiver. As the burly man looks shockingly at the receiver, Devon smiles.

"Hello. Ah Kazimir, how's Zarya? Of course, I was just telling Dmitri here that you'd say that."

Dmitri cautiously takes the phone from Devon *"Zdavstvuyte?* [Hello?] *Konechno.* [Of course.] *Da ser* [Yes sir]." Dmitri hands the phone back and then steps back.

"Yes, Kazimir, he did indeed. Thank you. You too. Goodbye." Devon hangs the phone up. "Now, Dmitri, right? You are going to take your men, get in your chopper, and fly away. Then next week, you will take your lieutenants here and go into the Triskelion Security Corporation, ask for Conner Fiore, He'll take care of everything. Am I understood?"

"*Da ser.*"

"You shall never again set foot on these premises without my direct order, I now lead the Obshchak, am I understood on this too?

"*Da ser.*"

"Then get out!" Devon yells, standing to his feet and slamming his fist on the table.

As soon as they are gone Devon whistles, at which Horrus howls. A few minutes later, the pack has returned to their leader, quickly followed by Xander and the guards.

"Xander, call Conner and TC to the conference hall. We have some things to discuss before the family gets here."

"All right," Xander says and leaves the room, returning shortly. "They're on the way. Mr. Gallagher and Mr. Jones are pulling into the extraction center as we speak."

"That's fine. Thank you Xander, go enjoy time with your family, I'll be along shortly."

As Xander leaves, Devon watches the CCTV as the chopper carrying Sean and Xavier lands. He gets up and heads out to the porch to greet them.

"Sean. Xavier. I wasn't expecting you so early but it's no problem, please come in. I have a meeting in a few minutes with my inner circle, but you all are of course welcome to enjoy the lodge."

"Ah, if we'd have known that we wouldn't have surprised you with our visit today for we need to have a discussion of our own," Sean states emphatically.

"Then let's do that now before the others arrive."

Devon leads the group into his private conference hall only large enough for five people to meet comfortably. After they get sat down, Sean looks at Xavier, who nods his head.

"Devon, we hear rumors that you're getting out. Before we've even started?"

"No, I'm not getting out… per se. I'm stepping back. I believe it's the best decision for Victoria and our children."

Sean and Xavier both take a minute to catch on. "Wait, Victoria's? Now? But Nicholas' only…"

"I know. Yes now, and I feel that this life will distance me extremely from them and growing up the way I did, I'm not going to let them feel like I'm not around or supporting them, I've already taken too much time away from my family. When Nicholas is fifteen, I'll probably try to take back the reins, and they'll all be trained as soon as they can in self-defense. This is not their legacy unless they choose it to be."

"Well, Devon, you're already a better father by making that decision and I'll fully support this."

"Thank you. To that end, supporting me, I want to be kept up to date on things, and I want to return. So, at the end of the week, I'll divide my controlling shares to you all, and step down to lead the logistics division within Triskelion Security, running that division remotely from my desk here. I need you all to make that push to the family and shareholders. If I divide my shares to you all, the person with the next most shares outside our circle would be Garmaggio, but he shouldn't be able to do anything without one of our guys' support, his share is that small. Now, I think my circle is here."

"OK, we can do that, and we just wanted to discuss it with you beforehand. Congratulations again."

As Sean and Xavier leave, Xander leads TC and OG in. Devon simply tells them straight up that he's backing down from being the boss, and instructs them to switch off every couple of years to keep anyone from trying to take out the family. He suggests, emphatically, that if one is in the office, the other should be in the field or at a remote office. He also informs them that Sean and Xavier know and are in the circle of credence and can be relied on with sensitive information. Lastly, before moving on, Devon requests to be kept informed of decisions, if not consulted about. They then go on to discuss other family affairs.

Later that night, when Devon finally emerges from his office, dreary eyed and tired, he's caught by Nicholas, his now three-year-old son, who was running by. Devon's eyes instantly light up and he smiles as he swipes him up, tickling him. Down the hall, Victoria turns the corner, trying to keep up.

"Hey, I got him, go to the bedroom. I'll be right there," Devon states.

"Are you sure, don't you have some big meeting tomorrow?" she says, raising an eyebrow.

"I'll tell you about it in a little bit," Devon says, kissing her.

As she walks away, Devon places Nicholas on the ground, "So, what book do you want to read tonight?"

"The lion one."

"Again, we've been reading that one for like a month now? I think we're near the battle though."

"Well Mommy doesn't like to read that one, she says it's too violent. And someone's not here to read it to me all the time." the little boy says with a smirk.

"Well I got a surprise for you, next week, Daddy's going to be here a lot more often."

"Really?"

"Do I lie to you?"

"No, sir. Daddy?"

"Yes, son?"

"I've missed you, I'll be glad if you're here more. Maybe we can swim more often."

"I think that's a great idea, but right now we have a book to read and some shut-eye to get, right?"

"Yes, sir."

Devon led his son to his room, prayed with him, guided him as he brushed his teeth, and tucked him in. Then read *The Lion, The Witch, and The Wardrobe* up to the end of the battle. He then kissed his son's head, pulled the blanket up a little and pulled the door until it was just slightly ajar. Devon then met Victoria in their room, he took a shower, changed into his pajama bottoms and climbed into bed beside his wife.

"I stepped down tonight. Starting next week, Conner is going to be acting CEO of Triskelion and Travis will be acting boss of the Gregorian family."

Victoria put her book down. "You did? So, what does that mean for us?" She looks intrigued.

"Well it's until Nicholas is fifteen, but nothing will really change, our expenses aren't that bad, we'll be bringing in a third of the profit of our family instead of a half, and the meetings will still be here, but I will not be required to do anything for them besides greet them."

"Devon, what about for actual work?" she says, worried.

"Oh, I'm going to be taking control of the logistics division of Triskelion, but I'll set it up to where I can work from my office here. I'll still have to call in for the board meetings every afternoon, but I'll be here."

"That's wonderful honey," Victoria says, kissing him.

The next week, Devon walks into the conference room, where the Triskelion Security board of directors had gathered. As he enters, everyone stood.

"Good afternoon everyone. As I'm sure you are all aware by now, I will be stepping down today, chief communications officer, Conner Fiore, will be stepping up to take over my role. To take his place, Gerald Cochran, our chief logistics officer will move into his role, and I will take Gerald's place as CLO, working from a remote office. The parties involved have all been consulted and are agreeable to this arrangement, as are a large contingency of our shareholders. I would like to thank all of you for embarking on this endeavor with us."

After the meeting, Devon returns to what was his office and empties his drawers and grabs the picture of him and Victoria from his desk, then heads to the helipad. As he is about to reach the elevator, Garmaggio comes up the stairs.

"Devon, I hear you are stepping down. I'm so sorry, if there is anything I can do to help, just let me know," he states, smiling coyly, as the elevator arrives.

"Please accompany me and we'll discuss it," Devon says walking onto the elevator. Garmaggio follows. "I am going from chief executive to chief logistics, any other move is of no concern to you unless I decide otherwise. Regarding the shares that just transferred, which I'm assuming told you of the events, any not sold to Travis and Conner were divided among the other bosses of the Maretelli family. Any move against this company or my family in my absence will be considered an attack on my personal life, and treated likewise. Good day." Devon steps off the elevator and heads for the waiting chopper.

As Devon looks back toward Garmaggio, he's smiling, and the doors close on the elevator. Devon gets on the chopper, and leans into the cockpit.

"If you and Garmaggio have any sneaky moves you plan on making I'd seriously consider that I have eyes both on your wife and children as well as your mother and father. If Xander doesn't hear from me within the hour, he has orders to 'step in'."

"Yes, sir." As they rise into the air, Devon stays standing, holding onto a strap.

At two hundred meters, Devon hears the pilot whispering something. "Mother, Lucy and Caleb, forgive me." Devon rushes to grab a parachute and dive out of the chopper, holding onto only his picture of Victoria, as the pilot presses a button and an explosion rocks the chopper as Devon enters the free fall toward the building. Devon curls his body right before slamming into the building, and rolling across the roof, slams into the rooftop access stairwell wall. Devon hears the elevator and sees several bodies, the last thing he remembers is hearing the faint sound of approaching boots. Then he passes out.

Two months later, a chopper flies over the Colorado mountains, landing beside the lodge. Travis and Conner both step out, surrounded by their guard details, they rush through the lodge into the makeshift hospital room that Antonin constructed following the crash. They surround a waking, yet still unresponsive, Devon.

"Xander, how's he doing?" TC asks.

"Well, at around four thirty this morning, we picked up faint signs of activity. When Victoria and I came in he was mumbling some and that's when we contacted you all. Victoria requested that I not contact anyone else until we get your opinions," Xander states, sliding his finger across a tablet with Devon's medical files.

"OG... T... C... what's... the... status?" Devon says between rasps.

"Sir, following your departure from the board meeting, we picked up surveillance video showing Garmaggio transferring funds. When we were able to track that to a chopper pilot we tried to call the flight crews, finding those communications offline, we grabbed the few trusted agents we could find and rushed to the roof, where we saw you impact the wall. We then had you airlifted here, and called Antonin and Xander to inform them of events so they could prepare for your arrival at the lodge. Conner and I then went to find Garmaggio, finding him speaking to a few of the board members, we returned to my office to plan out our next moves. We consolidated our allies and clientele before Garmaggio reached them and transferred all their files to a remote location Garmaggio doesn't know about   and have operated from there for a while. Then, about a week and a half ago, we secured Garmaggio's removal from the premises, revoked his shares and banned him from the building. Since then things have run smoothly," TC answers.

"Good… Call Sean and Xavier. We need to act fast," Devon says, pushing himself up.

"We," OG states, motioning between TC and himself, "have this handled. You need to relax and spend time with Victoria and Nicholas, they've been worried about you."

Devon grumbles, but he concedes the argument. He sits up. "Fine, but help me out of this bed, I'm not staying connected to this catheter nor confined to this bed," Devon says, disconnecting the tube running up his leg. He then gets up and heads to the closet, where Victoria placed some sweats and a T-shirt. Departing to the bathroom, where he gets changed.

Upon exiting the bathroom, he goes to his office and picks up the phone. OG rushes in and hits the dial tone. Devon glares at him and TC pries the phone out of his hand.

"In order to get authorization to take Garmaggio's shares and ban him, we had to sell the story that you were on long-term life support due to complications with treatment following the crash," OG states, tensing for the hit that was undoubtedly coming.

"Smart move. But maybe lead with that next time. Who knows the truth?" Devon wonders.

"The people in this lodge, our personal details, and Sean, Xavier and Antonin and their details. Everyone else thinks you're out of the game, and requested that TC and I maintain control of the company until a suitable leader can be found to hold the reins of the company. We've also tried to take out Garmaggio, but he went off the grid after we banned him," Conner claims.

"Ahh. Well thank you all. Please leave me in peace, so I can recuperate. This is a lot to hear."

Devon sits at his desk as the pair leave. When the door shuts and he sees the chopper lift off, he slams his arms on the desk and pushes everything off the desk. *Yelp!* Devon looks over. "Oh, I'm sorry Horrus." The German shepherd limped over to the corner away from Devon and curled into a ball. Devon slumps back into his desk chair, closing his eyes. He stirs out of that position when he hears the creak of a door, grabbing a pistol he points it at the door. Victoria comes into view and he puts the pistol down. She comes around the desk and starts kissing him, then takes his hand and leads him to the bedroom. Horrus stays in the corner.

That afternoon, Devon is in his office, working on the charitable foundation he decided to start, when Nicholas runs past the door, then comes back and peers around the door.

"Daddy! You're up!"

"I am. How was preschool?"

"It was good. Can we play a game?"

"What kind of game do you want to play?"

"Tag!"

"Tag? I don't know, do you have any homework?"

"No."

"What about chores? Is your room clean?"

"No chores, and my room is clean," Nicholas says with a super big smile.

"Hmmm. That face says otherwise, will I have to take away your TV privileges between dinner and bedtime?"

"Fine, it's not," Nicholas confesses.

"Well then let's go do that and then we'll play tag until it's time for dinner," Devon says following his son as he runs out of the office toward his room.

Chapter 10

Dad! DAD!" Nicholas, now fourteen years old, shouts, walking through the lodge.

"Nick, I'm in my office. What do you need?" Devon says putting books back on their shelf, with Adonis, the new alpha, standing alert.

Horrus had passed away when Nicholas was eight years old, Adonis was his son and just as agile. The rest of the pack followed their leader in the months following, leaving Adonis with a new group to rally.

"Can I have a few friends over later?"

"They're already here, aren't they?" Devon looks at his son, with a knowing look. "Finish your chores and make sure your brother and sister are doing their chores. Then I don't mind, but you know you need approval from both of us."

"I know, Dad, Annelyse is talking with Mom now. My room is clean, as is the bowling alley and movie theater, and Daniel and Charlotte are already working on their rooms," Nicholas says, handing the last book to his dad.

Devon thanks him, places it and pats the side of his leg, signaling for Adonis to follow, as he walks with his son toward the great room of the lodge.

"Later tonight, we need to talk in my office, son, after dinner maybe?"

"Does it have to be tonight?"

"Yes!"

"Then after dinner works fine," Nicholas says, patting his dad on the back, before jogging to the kitchen as Xander approaches.

"Time's up, Dev?" Xander asks.

"Yeah, as of tomorrow, I'm officially back and king of the American underworld once more. But for today, I'm still just Devon Gregory, devoted father, husband and the most prominent anonymous philanthropist there is," Devon says as they enter the great room.

Both of their families were spread out below. Nicholas welcomed his two best friends at the glass doors, and Xander's family was gathered around the TV watching the highlights of last night's games. Victoria and Grace were laughing with Nick's girlfriend, Annelyse, in the kitchen as they cleaned up from breakfast.

Devon approaches his wife in the kitchen.

"Good morning, Annelyse. Ladies, breakfast was amazing!" Devon kisses his wife on the cheek, then whispers, "When you get a minute, I need to talk to you in private."

"Good morning, Mr. Gregory," Annelyse responds as Nick arrives at her side.

"Grace, do you think you could finish up here? Devon and I need to chat," Victoria asked.

"Of course, Vic, Xander will help me finish up here."

Devon leads Victoria back to the office. At the door, Devon clenches his fist by his side, telling Adonis to lay in front of the door after both are in the office. As Devon turns around from closing the door, Victoria looks up from the files on his desk.

"Tomorrow's the day?" She asks solemnly.

Devon could already see the tears welling up in her eyes. "I'm afraid so, baby, and it's Nick and his friends' first day at their internships there. I know you're nervous about it, but I'll be OK." Devon feebly attempts to calm her.

"You don't know that. Look at the last time you left there, you almost died. YOU. ALMOST. DIED," Victoria weeps, beating onto his chest.

"Look at me. Victoria Alvarez Gregory, look at me!" She pulls her head up and looks at his face. "I love you. Nothing bad is going to happen to me or our son. I promise," Devon assures her, leaning down to kiss her. In response, she jumps up into his arms and sits on the desk and they continue kissing.

Xander approaches the door as lunch is about to start. Before he can knock, Adonis jumps up and the door opens to reveal Devon and Victoria walking out, Devon fixing his shirt and Victoria brushing her hand through her hair. Xander smiles, and turns around.

"Did you need something Xander?" Devon inquires.

"Just coming to get you both for lunch," Xander says, rolling his eyes.

"Lunch? Oh my, is it already that time?" Victoria asks in shock.

"Yes, ma'am, and everyone is waiting for you," Xander responds as they enter the great room to see everyone sitting around the table.

"Get it, Mr. G," Nick's friends say as they approach the table.

Nick gets up and heads for the bathroom, stopping by his father on the way. "Dad, zip it up!" he whispers.

Devon zips it up and takes his seat at the head of the table flanked by Xander's family on one side and his family, and their friends, on the other, with Victoria at the other end.

After a wonderful lunch of assorted hoagies, Nick and his friends retire to the movie theater, Xander's kids go to the bowling alley, Charlotte and Daniel go to the swimming pool and the ladies retire to the hot tub, while Devon and Xander clean up from lunch. They then join their wives for a little while.

About mid-afternoon, everyone is gathering in the great room. Nick is saying goodbye to his friends, while Annelyse stays on the couch. After saying goodbye to his friends, Nick sees his dad returning to the room.

"Dad. Can I talk to you alone please?"

"Sure, son, I was just about to go on a run, if you want to join."

Devon and Nick change into some shorts and sleeveless T-shirts and then head to the gym. As they run Nick keeps wavering across the path.

"Whoa, whoa. Let's take a break," Devon says, pretending to catch his breath. "What'd you want to talk about?"

"How do you know if someone is cheating on you?"

"Oh! Well, it's all about their reactions. Why? Do you think Annelyse is?"

"I don't want to, but it'd explain something that happened earlier."

"Ah. Well, I can't tell you what to do in that exact situation, but I'd think and pray about it. I'd only see two options: approach her about it, or just end things immediately. Either way, son, you need to address that, because just knowing what I do know, I'd say something happened, but I don't know what that thing would be."

"Thanks, Dad. I'll think it over. I bet I can beat you in three laps," Nick says and takes off.

"Oh no you don't!" Devon exclaims and runs after him.

As they come from their rooms after showering and changing, they banter about the race and who won.

"You totally cheated, you tried to trip me!" Devon protests.

"Listen, old man, if you can't keep your feet on the ground, don't blame me," Nick jests.

"Oh, the age card really, pulling the age card? Now that's dirty!" Devon says as they come toward the great room.

"Hell no!" Nick says, rushing down the steps. Everyone is asleep except Annelyse and Xander's sixteen-year-old son, Victor. Who are both skinny dipping.

Devon walks over to Xander, shakes him up and points over to the pool, where they pull Victor out into the pool house, while Nick is escorting Annelyse out of the pool, wrapping her in a robe, and taking her to the door.

"Nickie, please. It's not what you think," Annelyse pleads as Nick grabs her bag and clothes off the couch, takes her arm and leads her toward the door.

"I didn't want it to be so, but I just saw you! Don't tell me it's not what I think, we're done. Goodbye, guards make sure she gets home safe, then delete that address and number from all our logs please."

"Yes, sir, Mr. Gregory," one of the guards says, taking the bag and leading her toward the chopper, as Nick slams the door and then rushes toward the pool house.

As he approaches, his dad intercepts him. "Dad! Move! This doesn't concern you."

"When you asked me about it, it became my concern. Now if you don't stop I'm going to have to stop you, and that means hurting you."

"Try! How can I feel worse? Now MOVE DAD!"

"I'm sorry son," Devon says before hitting him in the shoulder and knocking him to the ground. "I'll let you confront him but do it with a calm head. You're madder at

Annelyse anyway, she incited it. Victor's just a boy, he just responded the same way any other guy would if a pretty girl was around."

Nick gets up and brushes himself off. Then he uses the skills he learned about calming himself from his martial arts training.

"OK, Dad, I'm ready."

"Nick, I need you to remember, whatever you do, he's been training with Triskelion agents for nine months, so he's not a simple bully with no training."

"I know, Dad, you wrote the training codes for Triskelion before you left. I've grown up with the best source of that training," Nick says as the enter the pool house.

Xander turns, Devon motions him to get out of the way.

"Guys work this out, and then come back inside for dinner."

Devon closes the door as he and Xander leave, and they hear things break on the other side. They go back in the house, turn on a movie, send an agent for pizza, and relax as their sons work out their issue. After an hour or so, Xander turns to Devon.

"Are you sure that was the best solution?"

"Let's find out!" Devon asserts, standing up.

The two dads cautiously approach the door to the pool house which is silent as a church in prayer. Devon turns the handle, while Xander pushes the frame. The door swings open to reveal the two boys battered and bruised, passed out on the floor, and surrounded by shattered furniture and equipment.

"Like a charm. They'll wake up after a while and we'll be as near to normal as we can get." Devon confirms.

A few hours later, Nick walks into the great room from the pool house and grabs some cold pizza. As he sits at the island to eat it, Devon comes in and spots his son.

"Feel any better?" Devon asks.

"I'm not as furious at Victor, but it doesn't mean I'm better. Where is everyone?" Nick says.

"In bed, Nick, you have been knocked out all night. It's midnight. Your mother is furious at me for not waking her. Son, you won't be better for a while, but look at it this way, you are up before Victor."

"Yeah, I am, aren't I?"

"You won that round, and that's impressive. Also, we need to talk, let's go to the office," Devon says, turning and motioning for his son to follow.

"You want me to put the pizza away?"

"No, we'll leave it out, just in case Victor wakes up before morning." When they enter the office, Nick sits down.

"No, not this one, son," Devon corrects as he enters a code on his phone and pulls down the leather-bound edition of *Chronicles of Narnia*, the one Nick always wanted but could never touch.

Nick stands and follows his father into a secret office hidden behind a bookcase. This one is much smaller, yet cozier than the other one. Sitting in the room are all his uncles, Xavier, Sean, Travis, Xander and Conner. Devon flips the top of a freestanding globe up, takes out two glasses and pours some scotch for him and his son. Everyone else already has their chosen drink.

"Son, you know that you start your internship tomorrow, but that also means I will be returning as CEO of Triskelion."

"I know, Dad. You'll be gone a lot more."

"Yes, but it also means that things are going to get a lot more dangerous too. You see, Triskelion is just a cover for my real operation. I work running one of the largest criminal enterprises in the nation, the Gregorian family, an extension of the Maretelli syndicate. Your uncles, Sean and Xavier, are part of the syndicate too."

"Yeah, sure Dad, and Cesare Garmaggio is your best friend."

"Actually, he's my bitter enemy. Wait, how do you know that name?"

"He's the greatest mobster in the nation, every organization known to man respects him. You're going to be booting him from office tomorrow."

"What?" Devon says, looking to his lieutenants, who avert their eyes.

"Yeah. He's the current CEO of Triskelion Security, as of four years ago, when he bought out the shares of Uncle Conner and Uncle Travis."

"All right son, listen intently to what I'm about to say. None of this leaves this office. Do not speak of it, or even think about it unless I bring it up."

"Yes, sir."

"All right. Salut!" Devon says, giving Nick the glass and raising it in the air, before gulping it down.

Nick tries to take a drink and nearly spits it all over the walls, before coughing. "Uhh."

"Oh yeah. I forget, it's an acquired taste. Don't tell your mom."

Devon places the glasses on the small table in the meeting room and leads his son out and to his room.

"Nick, you can go there whenever you want but no one else is allowed back there but you and I. Am I understood?"

"Yeah, I got it, Dad. No one else. G'night."

"Goodnight, son, see you bright and early in the morning." Devon then storms back into the office.

"You gave out to Garmaggio and didn't tell me? Are you mad?"

"I can explain," Conner says.

"We have a lot to discuss!" Travis adds in.

"Yes sir. And Devon…" everyone else says.

"Yes?"

"It's good to have you back."

"Get out. I'm not back yet, and you better be glad about that. Right now, I need to sleep or I'll lose it." Devon exclaims.

Devon follows them out, goes and puts the pizza away. Seeing the box open tells him that Victor did get some, and he heads to bed.

Chapter 11

The next morning Devon and his family had just finished breakfast when the door opened and his partners entered to cheering from Devon's children, who were excited to see their 'uncles'. As Victoria rose to greet them Devon glared and shook their hands. After a short reception, Devon excused them to the conference room off his office. After closing the door, Devon turned and attempted to act calmly, failing.

"You gave Garmaggio our company? What happened to him being banned from the premises?" Devon shouts, infuriated.

"Let me explain what's happened in the past decade since you left the scene," TC says.

The week after TC was officially named interim CEO, he was sitting in what was Devon's office, when several aides came into the office and clicked the TVs that lined the wall dividing a conference space from where the desk sat.

"Sir, we have a situation occurring on multiple fronts, it first occurred in Chicago, then we received reports from

New York, Miami, LA, Denver, Las Vegas and Dallas," the aide with the most seniority informed him.

"Well, what's the situation?" Travis says trying to track all that was happening on the screens.

"Just coming in now: reports of similar events in Moscow, Rome, Paris, London, Tokyo, Sydney, Cairo and Madrid," someone was telling the chief aide.

"Sir, what do we need to do? Your call," the senior aide asks, looking expectantly.

"First what is happening in those cities?" TC asks.

"Sting operations, sir, at least one of our operatives in each of these locations is reporting law enforcement interference in their affairs in New York, Russia, Rome, and Tokyo, were receiving multiple calls. We need a response, sir!"

"Code Black. Suspend all operations for seventy-two hours, system wide. I don't want to hear of a single infraction by any of our clients, if anything occurs, kill the contract and pull our forces back."

"ALL RIGHT EVERYONE, YOU HEARD THE BOSS. WE ARE NOW ON CODE BLACK! I REPEAT THIS IS A CODE BLACK SITUATION!" the chief aide says, into his headset as he's walking out followed by his companions, who were contacting their associates in all the different departments as well.

TC sat back and tried to breath and get through the meetings and conference calls for the next three days, anxiously awaiting word on the takedown. He'd scanned the news stations and the furthest he could piece together was that an anonymous source gave the FBI and INTERPOL records that indicated headquarters and safe houses for most of the major players on the international black market. However, he had no information on any of his contracts. Just as he was about to yell to his secretary, an aide rushed in with a packet of compromised locations, contracts lost, and assets in custody. The file was larger than a legal text book.

"These are all our contracts, assets and properties lost?" TC wonders.

"No, sir, this is all assets, families, and properties seized worldwide, ours are highlighted and we have that file being compiled now for records. I figured you'd want to know as soon as possible so I just brought you the whole report," the aide said.

"Ah. Very well. Bring me a copy of the file for my office records, when it's done," TC says.

The aide nods and leaves the room. Travis flips through the large stack of papers and is glad and impressed to see that he only lost two contracts, five assets, and twenty properties in the massive takedown out of the literally thousands of named families, hundreds of thousands of agents, and millions of properties. He then called the main offices in each of the cities involved and asked for full reports on activities and the situation from each of the contracts in all the areas. He needed the confirmation of their commitment to the company.

The next few months went by without too many incidents worthy of note, picking up a client here, reducing funds to a sector there. It was for the most part a smooth operating time for the company. Then around the start of TC's second year as acting CEO, he received a call from James Callehann, CEO of Phoenix Security based out of Ireland, who made TC aware of a recent decline in contracts.

Travis personally marched down to the legal department and asked to be escorted to who had control over record-keeping on contracts. Upon entering the designated location, TC asked for an explanation as to the reason he had to receive this information from a partner security firm.

"Well, sir," the aide responded. "We were tracking the contracts and when people started forcing our units out and denying our services in a number of areas nationwide, we informed Alexis Stanley, the chief legal officer, of the development and were expecting to hear from you. Why she didn't tell you is beyond me, sir."

"Very well, from here on out, inform Ms Stanley and send someone to inform my office as well, Thank you. So I'm giving you an honorary promotion to contractual aide to the CEO."

"Yes, sir, Thank you!" the aide says.

Travis then marches down to Alexis Stanley's office and demands to know why she failed to inform him of the recent decrease in contracts.

"Mr. Richards, I did not inform you of these developments because I have them well handled within my own department. I assure you, you have no need to be worried about these withdrawals," Ms Stanley says.

"Well, Ms Stanley, if you have them so well handled why do other firms know of our loss of clientele?"

"I can only assume that it is because our former clients have gone to them. You'd have to take that up with them."

"I'm well caught up with them, thank you."

"Well then, I'm afraid, I can't give you an answer."

Travis then walks out, aware of the point that she will offer him no more insight. As soon as he returns to his office he calls Conner to inform him of the developments. As soon as he gets off the phone with Conner, he receives word from SSG Transportation and Shipping, who inform him that they've had a number of their shipments get hijacked by unknown forces. When that conversation ended, Xavier Jones called him and said that he's had security disputes from various locations about suspicious characters and increasing hostility within his clubs. Travis struggles with each of these issues individually, and only when Conner arrives at the office can he make sense of what's happening.

Conner Fiore walked into the CEO office of Triskelion Security after receiving a call from Travis about the loss of contracts. He sees that Travis is having trouble dealing with all these individual problems, so Conner advises that he sees it as one large problem. That then becomes the basis for their claim to the board of directors calling for the immediate dismissal of several board members.

Once they started putting the issues together they saw a common thread throughout, for someone to be able to successfully make business relationships turn from stone to sand, would take someone with intimate knowledge of the client and contractor. For shipments to be so easily hijacked would take basic understanding of the transport security detail used by SSG, designed by Triskelion, and in order to cause disturbances at multiple locations of Jones' industry within a certain distance from each other would mean knowing all the cover locations, used within a particular region, also created by Triskelion. Meaning that the person behind all of these issues was an enemy or rival of Triskelion Security and would need access to Triskelion records.

The only person who could possibly be at this stage of the company's development would be Garmaggio. Toss that together with the fact that he'd need valid passcodes in order to access all those logs, since their chosen route, detail and operation location change on a daily basis, would mean that either someone slipped him codes or someone forgot to remove his codes from one of the servers and with the way the servers are set up, get access to one, you have access to all. Combining this with what Ms Stanley said means that one or more individuals, and possibly high-ranking individuals, were working to get Garmaggio back within Triskelion's good graces. Considering all these things, TC and Conner both decided this is an issue that had to be dealt with immediately, therefore they called for the board of directors to meet without delay.

Once the entire board was called together, Conner and Travis took the time to see who would be friendly with Alexis Stanley, trying to get a read on who they could trust. Immediately, Alexis is approached by Clay Braddock, the man who replaced Garmaggio as chief strategic officer and who they considered a strong ally. Also joining the opposition was Zachery Snyder, chief operations officer, who was brought in on his skill with delicate matters to hold TC's spot while he was acting CEO. As the meeting began everyone was wondering why they were called.

"Ladies and gentlemen of the board, I know many of you are concerned with the reason we called you all here today. I found it disturbing to be called this morning by James Callehann from Phoenix Security, which as many of you know is our partner firm on the international scene. James informed me that we'd lost contracts. Upon investigating these contracts, I came across a larger issue that Conner, and myself, feel needs to be addressed urgently. There seems to be some question as to who operates the company on a day-to-day basis. I am acting CEO, so named by this board and the board of trustees and approved by the shareholders. That is not changing without a unanimous vote of this body, or a majority vote of the trustees or shareholders, as established in our guidelines at the foundation of this company."

"I'd like to raise a concern about the state of our affairs then?" says Clay.

"Very well," TC says, begrudgingly.

"I'm concerned you and your cohort are leading us asunder considering the recent events and the incident this morning where a former associate of ours attacked our interests in three different sectors. How could this breach of our forces have gone unnoticed?" Clay says dramatically, not realizing his mistake until late after the fact.

"Well, Mr. Braddock, for one I was not aware that it was an attack by a former associate of ours, but thank you for that and as to why it was not addressed sooner is probably because Mr. Fiore and I trusted that each of you would delete this associate's credentials from all our systems as soon as he was removed from the premises. Therefore, if a certain individual like Ms Stanley, who stated her contempt of my position this morning, and yourself, who is obviously against Conner and I, did not delete his credentials, and were let's say trying to rally support to oust myself and Conner from the company, which we helped found, from our positions on this board. You'd find it very hard to accomplish the second objective, even given the success of your earlier duplicity. This is because while we made sure to be amenable with most of this board, we also entrusted it to professionals, who are well versed in their vocations and acquainted with the business world. We do not intend, nor will we allow this company to be run like the mob. By comparison, if Garmaggio were here, he'd make suggestions that are fairly like Mafia rule, considering that before this, his entire life was his family within the Cosa Nostra."

"Aren't you all former military, Garmaggio, Conner, and yourself?" Braddock mentions.

"Yes, however Garmaggio left from within the ranks of the Special Forces division. When we, Conner, myself, and the late Devon Gregory left, we were in command of our divisions. Devon and myself held the same position, I took the mantle after he left, and we all had the opportunity to progress further up the chain of command, to become generals. Devon was even offered a position with the joint chiefs of staff but denied it to stay with his squad until one of our missions took too much of a toll and by then the position was filled. So yes we all have military experience, but obviously that shaped each of us differently. I would now like to call for the removal from the board of directors of Triskelion Security Corporation chief legal officer Alexis Stanley, chief strategic officer Clay Braddock, and chief operation officer Zachery Snyder, unless they can provide to the remaining board members reasons for their stay."

Mr. Snyder was shocked to hear that his name was mentioned, and after lengthy discussions, the board decided to remove Alexis and Clay, but that Zachery Snyder would be allowed to keep his position, citing that due to his innocence in the details of the coup, he was no real risk to the company. Following the removal of Ms Stanley and Mr. Braddock from the building, Travis asked for ideas on how they might be able to control the loss of contracts should it happen again. Conner offered the idea of an international conference of the criminal underworld. Travis liked the idea in the long term but wanted a short-term plan as well. Another idea was amending the contracts to include a clause that stated:

This contract cannot be breached with such-and-such a condition being met a particular set of specific events that the breach party has to confirm as exactly what happened to a joint session of trustee and director boards and have an overwhelming majority to get away scot-free, if that particular circumstance is not met they have to pay a certain amount of money to the company over a definite number of intervals or until their paid amount matches the amount spent on their contract.

Or something like that. Travis found this option appealing and asked for a consensus of opinions, then the board voted in both measures to amend the contracts and to begin the process of setting up an international conference of the criminal underworld.

For the remaining duration of his term, Travis Richards didn't face any real major problems, and when it came time to hand the reins over to Conner, he thought Conner would have an easy term as CEO.

Chapter 12

Little did Travis know that Garmaggio and his supporters were rallied and ready to invoke an even larger scandal over the next few quarters.

When Conner first sat in the CEO's chair, he felt that he had some major work ahead of him to do something that would mean anything to the company or the Gregorian family. After a couple of quiet weeks, Conner received a pile of packets that would create an avalanche of problems for his term.

One day, when Conner stepped into his office, there was a pile of contracts sitting on the corner of his desk. After sitting down and reading through his emails, he grabbed the first one and nearly spat his coffee all over the desk. The entire pile of packets were breach of contracts that he would have to look at and determine if they required him to call the joint session to discuss. Most did not, thanks to the new clause. A few lost contracts were commonplace every couple of years. Conner became aware of a larger situation when the next week more breached contracts appeared on his desk, and the next week, even more, and so on and so forth for nearly a month and a half. Conner knew that with this many contracts being lost, the company would not be able to stay afloat. To that end, he started calling the contract holders to see if there was something to be done. Most said that the only way they'd stay with Triskelion was if Garmaggio was positioned as CEO. Upon hearing that, Conner called Travis in and together they called every breached contract holder, most saying the same thing. Upon seeing this trend, Conner switched to calling the board of trustees, who had become aware of the situation and were rather concerned.

Conner decided that if the board of trustees was worried, he needed to get commitments from the shareholders' congress about not supporting Garmaggio. After hundreds of calls and hours of discussions and debates, the odds were bleak. During these calls and discussions, it dawned on Conner and Travis what had transpired in the past few months.

Ever since they'd removed Alexis Stanley and Clay Braddock, the two disrupters, with the help and contacts of Garmaggio, were contacting clients and shareholders of the company and spotlighting every chink, and wobble, and issue that had occurred since Devon's untimely 'death'. Alexis and Clay framed the events in such a way as to say that had Garmaggio been there, these issues wouldn't have occurred, which for the most part was true, although it would be because he was the one inciting most problems. The other issues are situations every growing business must deal with. After explaining this to most, some were won back over, but not enough to stop the plan in its tracks.

The next week, Conner asked to meet the board of directors at the original location of Triskelion Security, which Xavier Jones had turned into a private lounge, keeping the conference room upstairs. Eight out of the ten other members beside TC and himself arrived at the location. The other two members were too new to know the location and be trusted with the true identity of the company.

"Ladies and gentlemen, I've called you all here to discuss a certain matter that pertains to all of us. As I'm sure you are all aware, we've lost many contracts in the past months, so much so, that if we do not get new, or reconcile the old, contracts we are surely to be out of business. The issue with reconciling these contracts to us is that they will only submit re-entry with Garmaggio as CEO. Thus, I've struggled with making a decision."

"Why struggle? Bring Garmaggio back and get the old contracts," one of the members of the board proclaimed.

"Doing that would be ulterior to Devon Gregory's wishes."

"His wishes be damned, he's not here to concern us with them."

"And there's that can of worms I knew was coming," TC mutters, and Conner nods, smirking.

"Actually, that's why I've struggled. It's been undoubtedly decided that we need to give in to Garmaggio's demands, with that being decided I need to gather supporters to ensure that Garmaggio doesn't ramrod this board into any tumultuous situation and turn us into an extension of his power plays," Conner says.

"Isn't that what Devon did, creating the company?" Zachery Snyder asks.

"Watch what you say. Devon founded this company on the principle that it would stay above the frays of the political world. Our forces are contracted to do a job, we do that job and we leave no questions asked. Every contract we take on is reviewed by a board that reviews the political ramifications of our contract and prepares countermeasures for them, and sets guidelines for our forces to use. If these political issues arise and our forces do not follow the protocol set by that board, the team or member found working counter to our guidelines is then immediately pulled from the field and redeployed elsewhere, after undergoing recertification. Therefore, no, our company, as of right now, does not partake in political power plays, or any other kind of power grabs. Something Garmaggio would undoubtedly use it for. To protect the original purpose of this company I will need the support of most of this board. I say this with trepidation," TC answers.

"Why?"

"What I need is for you all to stand with me against Garmaggio in any matters that would work contrary to our purpose. The trouble is that it is a dangerous, somewhat fatal decision. It will not require all of you, just four or five to stand with myself and Mr. Richards. We will do our best to protect you by whatever means necessary, however, that does not mean that Garmaggio cannot reach you. Devon was well protected and Garmaggio still got to him. Luckily he failed in that endeavor," Conner explained.

It took a minute, then everyone realized what Conner said.

"Are you saying that?"

"Devon Gregory is alive and well. He's living in an undisclosed location and out of touch with most. Only Mr. Richards, myself, and his closest friends know where he is, how to get there and how to contact him. And even that changes weekly, if not daily. We had to give the impression that he had not survived to allow for the removal of Garmaggio from the board for the unsavory actions taken against Mr. Gregory."

After a long and tedious discussion, everyone was committed to maintaining the ideals and would vote for what was in the company's best interest regardless of Garmaggio's opinion, and would work to keep him in check if anything were to go wrong.

After returning from the meeting, Conner calls a press conference and announces that at the end of the fiscal year, he'd step down as CEO and allow the shareholders' congress to replace him. The shareholders' congress met immediately and elected Garmaggio, who after a couple months' observation, took full control over the reins of CEO of Triskelion Security. Luckily before he could take the reins, TC and Conner were successful in setting up the Interchange, the International Exchange of the Criminal

Underworld, with an Interchange champion who can regulate international criminal guidelines between Interchange meetings.

Chapter 13

Devon listens intently as TC and Conner explain. When Conner finishes Devon thinks for a minute.

"So technically, there is a way for me to gain my rightful spot back, and have more influence."

"Possibly, to participate in the melee, and have the potential for the title of Interchange champion, you need the endorsement of an established criminal family or entity. You also get to select two vice-contenders to participate in your stead, should you ever get winded or would like a break."

"Well obviously I would choose you all. How does the melee work?"

"Each region is cordoned off within the facility, Phoenix Security is donating one of their remote outposts for the location, the contenders from within specific institutions will face off one versus one until just one contender remains for the institution, then each region will do the same. After this, the contenders will enter the ultimate arena, for the grand melee, and face off in a free for all until just two individuals stand. After a brief recess for recuperation, the two finalist contenders will face off in the showdown, which only ends one of three ways: submission, unconsciousness or death. The winner is declared the Interchange champion and leads the conference that follows. Oh, and Dev, Nick signed up to participate this morning at like five forty-five, before registration for non-leaders ended."

"You're telling me my son, who is just now joining the Triskelion Junior Force, signed up for an expert level melee event, without proper authorization?"

"No, he had authorization. The highest authorization actually, he was personally recruited by Garmaggio."

"What? Xander, I need you to evacuate everyone now. We've been compromised."

"Wait, what?" Sean asks.

"Garmaggio knew my son would want to prove himself the best, so he gave him the opportunity to, which my son took. Giving Garmaggio access to our system and thus our location. We need to get below NOW!"

After emerging at their emergency bunker below the house, everyone can see each other and Devon approaches Nick.

"Son, did you sign up for an event called the Interchange championship melee?"

"Yeah, isn't it great Dad? An anonymous promotor sent me the link and backer info. Now I can show the world everything you taught me."

"Yeah, son. It's cool, please be careful. You might've gotten yourself in a little over the head though," Devon says before turning back to his friends.

"We need to get him knocked out early, but not too early. As soon as we reach the final ten from each organization, I want him taken off the court. Put us on the roster. As soon as the security team clears us, we're going in and taking Triskelion back."

"But how?" Xavier asks.

"Same way Garmaggio took it from us, politics. You four together have the next most share of Triskelion. To win, we need to use something Garmaggio doesn't value: honor. This will also allow me to disgrace him in the melee, because all other organizations worldwide see the value of personal honor. So Xavier you'll introduce a rule to create a code of honor for Triskelion which all individuals must adhere to in order to remain with the company. This code will be overseen by a committee of individuals from each department and led by two board members. The details are up to you, except the two board members you choose are from within our circle, and the code of honor is already an established doctrine, which allows for immediate implementation. After you make the motion, Sean will second it, as long as Travis, Conner and a couple others agree it will pass. Upon its implementation, you'll name Garmaggio for review and quickly and publicly disband him. Before he can even leave the office, Conner will rise and take control of the board, as all of this is happening I will be landing on the roof and coming down the elevator, passing Garmaggio as he is escorted out of the board room. Then Conner will offer me the seat of

CEO, which I will turn down, and then the board will vote to place me there anyway."

Everything goes according to plan, and after taking his place as CEO, Devon casts Garmaggio as a priority alpha-omega ten—extreme risk, vital to continuity of the company—immediate detainment. Knowing that he was on a warpath, all supporters of Garmaggio tried to flee, each was met with due restraint by loyal forces of the Triskelion Junior Force, led by the most experienced of forces, the first operatives of the Triskelion force, who Devon got at Fort Liberty.

With Devon back at the helm of Triskelion, preparations for the Interchange championship melee went exactly as TC had envisioned them when he created the event.

Chapter 14

It's been several months since Devon returned to Triskelion. Most of that time has been spent on readying everyone for the first ever annual Interchange summit. After a couple of nights of chatting, a formal ball would be held that would kick-off the event. The following day, skirmishes will start as the sun appears over the horizon of the Swiss Alps. From that point the fights will dictate everything. Hopefully getting through all the smaller ones on the first day, making the second day of fighting the last. The grand melee would end the fights and commence the meeting.

Devon is sitting at his desk in the middle of the logistics center, reading through last minute reports of supplies and personnel logs for the trip. Then, suddenly, all the screens in the logistics center start flashing red. Devon jumps up out of his chair, grabs the remaining files and quickly rushes out into the hallway and up the stairs to Conner's office, where he and TC are meeting to go over the last few details.

"Sorry to interrupt guys, but it's go time! We have just under four hours to make landfall at the site before the first of the other syndicates start arriving."

Both men nod and send the code to all essential personnel before heading for the helipad. On the rooftop they're met by Nicholas and his cadre of agents, who are in air security for the Big Triskeles, the three most powerful members of the Triskelion board of directors-CEO, CSO, and the CLO.

They landed two and a half hours later, on a helipad outside a grand resort. Waiting for them at the entrance was Nicholas' godbrother, Dominic Callehann.

"Uncle Devon, Father is sorry he couldn't make it, there was a situation with the other liaison for Phoenix Security, so father had to cover for him and clean up his mess."

"Dominic, not in front of my associates please, they're not too familiar with your father or family's situation. And tell your father, I understand. Now please, what is this place?"

"Right. Father purchased this place as the shareholders' safe zone in case of war. It is completely secluded from the rest of Switzerland, only accessible by air travel and an underwater cavern system. However, while father has no need of it yet, he has given you all permission to use the premises. He says he understands the consequences of such a deal and will deal with them when the time comes, whatever that means. Also, the property is high enough in the air to be considered international territory, as well as private property under my father's name. Before we bought and renovated it, it was a ski resort with an indoor water park for kids. We've since turned what was the waterpark into a stadium conference hall, with two hundred and seventy-five individual sponsor privacy boxes. It also furnishes five hundred elaborate rooms, twenty-five security rooms with a central security hub, and various other luxury amenities including bowling alley, pool, putting greens, massive three thousand-vehicle garage, dock, natural hot spring mineral pool, billiards hall, ten full service bars, multipurpose sports arena, and many others."

"Wow. When I asked James for a place I didn't realize he had this good of a hook-up."

"Well yeah, when you're the world's largest legitimate arms manufacturing and security firm, there's substantial profit to be made in collateral material."

"I see he gave you the pointers I advised when dealing with my incoming associates."

"Yes. Now, I must return to Africa for a coronation, but if you need anything Bryce Ortega is our general manager here and will be happy to see to any of your needs," Dominic says as a well-dressed man steps forward, a spitting image of his father.

"Ortega? You must be Lucian's boy."

"Yes, sir. Now, please allow our staff to show you all to your rooms, Mr. Gregory, and young Mr. Gregory, please follow me," Bryce says.

After everyone got settled and changed, they met back by the entry to welcome the first arrivals, the Yakuza representatives. After greeting their delegation, Devon introduced them to Bryce's appointed liaison for the duration of the use; each delegation was given a liaison, with Triskelion's liaison being Bryce himself. After the Yakuza's arrival, all the other delegations arrived shortly. Within three hours, most of the delegations were present with only the Bratva and Cupola groups yet to arrive. Soon thereafter, Devon invited everyone to dinner. Just before Devon closed the door, three large MI-24 'Crocodiles' landed outside the foyer. Devon motioned to TC, OG, and his son, given the moniker 'Hotshot' due to his fast rise in the Junior Force.

"*Zdrastvooyte* Pahkan! Welcome, allow me to introduce you to Alyosha, your liaison to the resort for the duration of your stay. Please allow him to show you to your room and when you're ready, join everyone for dinner, Alyosha will show you the way."

"*Bal'shoye spaseeba*," Kazimir Maksim Konstantinavich responded in thanks, following Alyosha as his billowing fur coat and two enormous guards follow. After he retreats around the corner, Devon and the others go to dinner.

Well into the meal, there's a commotion by the doors, and in busts Garmaggio leading the Cupola delegation into the room.

"What, Devon? No grand welcome for your old friend? That just seems rude." Immediately TC, OG,

Hotshot and the rest of the Triskelion forces rise and aim at Garmaggio. The Cupola forces whip out their weapons in response. For what seems like an eternity, Devon analyzes Garmaggio, Garmaggio analyzes Devon, and everyone else analyzes the situation. Then Devon lifts his hand.

"That's enough, put your guns down! NOW!" All the Triskelion forces drop their weapons and return to their seats. But TC, OG and Hotshot keep their eyes on Garmaggio and their hands on their weapon. "We're here on an agreement of peace for the melee, I will not have it broken in a couple hours by the very ones that developed the idea."

"Mr. Garmaggio, I'm gonna have to request that your men holster your weapons or I'll have to have you escorted from the premises. The owner's request is not to have any uninspected weapons on the property," Bryce asks politely.

"It's Don Garmaggio to you, of the Cupola. Gregory call your dog off before I punt him across the room," Garmaggio says smugly.

"Howard, just listen to the man. For one he's not my dog, he's the general manger here, and contrary to what you believe this is not my property. Its use was donated by a third-party affiliate and I wouldn't upset Mr. Ortega and his staff, they've all been trained by the Swiss military and Israeli Special Forces," Devon says calmly.

Garmaggio glares at Devon for addressing him by his civilian name, before motioning to his men to holster their guns, knowing Israeli Spec Ops is way out of his league.

The rest of the night is uneventful, just chatting and dancing the night away. With all the most dangerous men in the world gathered together in one place, no one dared disturb the peace again, only someone as brash as the former colonel, Howard Josephs, Don Cesare Ignacio Garmaggio would even attempt to do anything.

The next day the battles started, fierce battles within organizations happened first, whittling down the contenders from each division, all would return for the ceremonial melee in a couple days. Then came rivalry showdowns: Cupola vs. Commission, Bratva vs. Odessa, Yakuza vs. Triad, etc. The fiercest warriors came from the African tribesmen who banded into regional gangs, who pooled resources to buy into the grand melee. The next greatest threat was the Bratva, certainly the most gruesome fighters. The Yakuza were the most refined warriors. The Triad sported the best equipped warriors. However, everyone knew this melee was mainly an international stage for the final showdown between Devon Gregory, and his honorable Triskelia, and the Cupola backed Garmaggio.

After another day of skirmishes. Everyone retired to recuperate for a few hours. At 16.48 hours, the melee resumed. All the non-combatants were in their assigned privacy boxes, watching. All the combatants were gathered on the arena floor, with weapons decorating the tables and wall section behind them. At seventeen hundred hours, they're left with what's holstered on their person or in their hands. Much to his disappointment, Nicholas was watching from the safety of the Triskelion privacy box, where TC and OG joined him. The plan was for them to switch out with his dad, however, things didn't go as smoothly with their fights and when the smoke cleared, only Devon was well enough to handle the melee, and therefore had no alternates.

Devon glances at the clock hanging above the arena floor, 16.47.45. He has fifteen seconds to analyze his weaponry and determine what to stash where. He'll need the guns but can't have the cartridges exposed, he'll keep them stashed beneath his Kevlar. Fourteen seconds. The kunai will be valuable in taking out the most opponents with the least effort, but where to stash them for ease of access? The straps holding his vest together seem to have the perfect openings between vertical stitching to hold the kunai, and will also allow for better protection if layered correctly. Thirteen seconds, the war hammer and broadsword are his specialty, but they are too heavy to holster and he can't carry both: those are out. Devon sees two tomahawks; he can slip those beside his guns. Ten seconds. Beside the tomahawks is a two-piece bo staff that can slip into the sleeves at the small of his back. Five seconds, got it! Two short swords laying on the table. The buzzer sounds. Devon quickly holsters as many weapons as he could. He spent most of his time on the kunai, layering forty-five of them across his abdomen. Lastly, he grabs the two short swords and slips them into the sheaths crossing his back. He turns around and sees that a lot of the individuals are still assessing their cache. However, on the other side of the arena stands his arch nemesis sharpening a bowie knife, Devon turns around, slips a couple of tanto knives in his vest, throws a couple whetstones into his pocket and grabs a trench knife. He turns around as the clock shows ten seconds until the melee begins.

Devon closes his eyes and takes a deep breath, as he slowly exhales, he listens carefully for shifting footfalls, erratic breathing, any behavior to determine where everyone is planning to strike. As the alarm blares signaling the start, Devon opens his eyes. Three assailants are rushing toward him, he flips three kunai out and tosses it at them, nailing each of them in the shoulder. Then out of nowhere a heavy battle axe swings by and decapitates them simultaneously. Devon takes a step forward, tossing kunai in every direction, hitting pressure points on people left and right and making them collapse. When his abdominal holsters are emptied of kunai he pulls the two-piece bo staff out, and knocks contender after contender unconscious without losing a step. Suddenly he stops, places two ends of the bo staff together to form one bo staff, as combatants surround him. He breaks out and they all try to stop him. After knocking three rows of them back, he loses the staff. He quickly loads a pistol and fills the other hand with a tomahawk. Crossing his hands, he slowly advances, shooting people in the wrists and shoulder. Anytime someone gets too close he either nicks them with the blade end of the tomahawk or knocks them with the blunt end. Suddenly he collapses, his heel being sliced open. He patches it up and closes his eyes.

"Uh oh!" OG says looking at TC with a worried look.

"What, Uncle Conner?"

"He's going blood vision," TC says pulling Nick back to explain. "You know your father has an extreme distaste for severely hurting people, but when he goes blood vision, he loses the ability to control that. He's not experienced it since his days with the Rangers, and even then, it was a rare event. What I'm saying is, you're probably not going to want to see this, and if you do see it, you will not be able to forget it. So, think carefully before walking back onto the box."

Back on the arena floor, Devon opens his eyes and all he sees are black figures. He drops his gun, grabs the other tomahawk and just attacks everyone in the vicinity. He swings to his left, and brings his tomahawk across the bare chest of an assailant. He spins to the right and brings the tomahawk down on someone's head, knocking them out. He swings the other one low and knocks two more assailants off their feet before bringing the blunt end down on their chest, collapsing their lungs. By the time the alarm sounds again, signaling the end of the grand general melee, only five people remain conscious and well enough to fight in the championship: Don Cesare Garmaggio of the Cupola, Devon Gregory of the Commission, Andrei Mendelevich of the Bratva, Akida Tomiji of the Yakuza, and Abimbola of the African syndicate. At this exact time, Devon stands to his feet and opens his eyes. The arena is silent, taking in the number of injured as attendants move the fallen contenders to a makeshift med bay to nurse them back to health. Then the groups retire for the evening. The next day is the grand championship melee, only one can come out on top, but the real question is will Devon, bound by his honor, be able to take down the manipulative nature that gives Garmaggio his strength?

Devon wakes up the next day, and tends to his bandages after a long hot shower. He then calls Victoria and has a lengthy conversation catching up on everything the other has missed in the couple of days they've been apart. After affixing his gear back on, he taps on the door for the guarded escort each champion is receiving to the arena. As he enters the arena, the assembled bodies are cheering for their champion.

The melee begins the same as the previous one, with an arsenal of weapons behind each champion that they've requested. Devon chose specialty types of each of the weapons he carried yesterday, except the kunai. After equipping the new weapons, he turned and studied each of his opponents, assessing their performance yesterday. Garmaggio barely moved yesterday, probably made deals with other participants to conserve his energy for the inevitable showdown. Andrei specialized in overpowering his opponents, using brute force to make them crumble. Akida relied on speed and accuracy to catch his opponent off guard; he was responsible for Devon's severed tendon in his ankle. Abimbola utilized fear by crying out fiercely as he attacks, hoping to shake up his opponent. Devon had proven himself yesterday, and everyone knew it. They were expecting him to sit back and let the other champions knock each other out until it was just him and Garmaggio; they didn't know him very well.

As the melee started, everyone did as he expected, rush toward each other besides him and Garmaggio. Garmaggio just stood in the corner waiting. Devon however approached slowly. The first to notice him was Akida Tomiji who tried to move swiftly to attack his ankles but Devon quickly spun his bo staff, tripping Akida. As he rose to his feet with a special kunai in his hand, Devon and he had a short skirmish before Devon swept him off his feet again and bashed his head on the arena floor, and pushed him out the way. After Akida, Abimbola was about to finish off Andrei when he saw Devon. Feeling that Andrei was no longer a threat he turned to attack Devon, screaming at him fiercely as predicted. Devon calmly approached and disarmed and struck Abimbola down, afterwards removing earplugs and asking if he was saying something. Lastly Andrei stood to his feet. A good six inches taller than Devon he was a formidable opponent if faced first, but being battered previously, Andrei was already sore. As he approached Devon he limped. Devon considered a way to attack first before getting overpowered. Deciding there was no better, quicker option Devon spun into a roundhouse kick, hitting Andrei in the face, knocking several teeth out as well as knocking Andrei himself unconscious. Finally, it was the showdown everyone had been waiting for: Devon Gregory vs. Cesare Garmaggio.

After a brief reprieve for lunch, everyone reassembled in the arena. Devon loosened up while Garmaggio just stared at him. The match started and both men approached the center, firing shots at each other with each step. Devon came out with a shot in the arm, Garmaggio with one in the shoulder. They threw their guns away and each pulled a sword out and swung. Metal clashed as their swords met each other. Swing after swing sounded throughout the arena as each man parried the other's attack for a few minutes. Then Devon swung and Garmaggio's blade snapped in half and he had a slight cut on his cheek. Garmaggio threw down his sword and pulled out his bo staff, Devon quickly matched him. They danced across the arena each landing a couple blows on the other but in the end, Devon's bo staff proved to be the superior weapon, splintering Garmaggio's wooden bo staff. Following that each grabbed their custom-made knives and resumed the fight. Slash after slash commenced and each came away with fresh cuts to their arms and chest, the final melee being an armor-less battle of skills. Eventually Devon tired of his knives and threw them away, Garmaggio doing the same out of respect for tradition. The skirmish ended with a fit of hand to hand combat. Garmaggio headlocks Devon, who then rolls and traps Garmaggio with his body into releasing him. Punches fly hitting cuts or gunshot wounds. However, Garmaggio's injures prove to be too much for him, being taken to the ground and pinned with a specialty move Devon invented while reworking the training handbook for Delta Squad.

Devon rises as victor of the melee, but as he turns to receive applaud by organizations and other participants, he removes his eyes from Garmaggio. Garmaggio seizes the opportunity to unveil a hidden blade and tries to stab Devon. Shouts of horror resound, as Devon spins, knowing Garmaggio to fight dirty, and disarms him and places him in a specialty headlock, pinning his arms behind him. Two guards approach and detain him, but stay on the arena floor. Bryce approaches Devon and states that the various representatives wish to meet to discuss the fight.

"Very well. Thank you, Bryce, tell everyone that we're adjourned until after dinner."

"Of course," Bryce says.

Devon walks to the main conference room where bosses are arguing over the event, some even accusing the whole Cupola for the actions of their representative champion. Devon enters and all silence themselves.

"Gentlemen, obviously I know that this upsets you all. However, we cannot blame the entire organization for the actions of one of their representatives. However, I do admit we need to work out what we need to do about him. We also need to discuss details of what the champion now means. I hope none of you mind but I dismissed our assemblies until after dinner so we can have time to discuss these things now. If you all would like to call your underboss and enforcer, or consigliere, or most trusted advisers to join us. I think that would be best."

After everyone is gathered, Devon requests that they commence with the meeting. "First things first, we need to handle this situation with Garmaggio."

"Why do 'we' need to do that?" Kazimir states.

"Well, Pahkan, I've exhausted all of the American resources I can afford to use on handling him, which got him to flee to the Cupola in the first place. Also, with his actions here today, if we do not do anything we set precedent for other individuals who have no honor."

"That explains why they need to get involved with this Garmaggio fellow, but why must I he's not hurting the Yakuza," Nishioka Fujimaro, the obuyan of the Yamaguchi Gama, the ranking gang of the Yakuza states.

"Not yet, Kumicho, using the Japanese title for 'supreme kingpin', but he will, his ambition is ceaseless. I'm sorry to speak out of turn but if you were not to agree I could always invoke the code of jingi."

"Very well. You have my support, American," Fujimaro states.

"Good. Now I cannot be privy to this conversation, therefore I will need to confirm a representative to look out for my group's interests. To that extent I choose Bryce Ortega, he's well suited to look after my interests and witnessed the events thus far committed by Garmaggio here. TC, please go retrieve him. Now, on the conclusion of the Garmaggio business, I will return and Bryce will leave, not to be bothered until we are finished with our business," Devon explains, everyone nods and OG and Devon exit the room.

TC is speaking with Bryce outside the room. Devon explains what he would like to happen, and gives him a brief rundown on how to speak to these men. After this, Bryce enters the room and doesn't leave for two hours. Upon his exit, he shakes Devon's hand and returns to work, while Devon and the others return to the room.

"With that out of the way, I would like to request that we discuss what follows the grand melee for the champion. In my opinion I believe he should be granted entry into our organizations and placed in charge of the Interchange for a duration of three years."

"That's unacceptable. Our organizations are close-knit brotherhoods that require extensive personal experience to be granted membership. As Pahkan, the Russian Mob refuses to bestow that honor on anyone we've not tested," Kazimir states standing in outrage.

"I understand, so please take your seat so we can reach a more amenable solution." Kazimir glares at Devon as he sits. "Since you feel that way Kazimir, what do you suggest we do to remedy the situation?"

"I'm unsure."

"Can anyone think of a way to remedy the issue the Pahkan has presented?"

"We could each offer a test, or trial, which would grant them the ability to join our organizations, but not without proving their worth," Nishioka counters.

"That is reasonable, Pahkan?"

"I can agree to this, but since we are placing a condition for our safety, perhaps we should place one for the champion's protection as well. Say, when he joins he's given rank of captain, or equivalent status, that way members can't easily overstep his decrees," the Pahkan states.

"Sounds good," Devon says, "Anyone have anything else to add?"

"On the plains of Africa, kings and such have honor guards composed of representatives of all the tribes he leads. We do this for our champion is my condition," Abimbola states, as representative of the African syndicate.

"Nice, a detail of forces from each of the organizations within the Interchange. We can each submit a list of candidates and they can choose one of each organizations' candidates to add to his 'honor guard'. How would you all feel if we also each provide an adviser so that the champion doesn't dictate policy that doesn't favor all?"

Everyone is nodding their head.

"Alina, you are the last that hasn't given a condition or reward, do you have any ideas to present?"

"I would suggest that we give him a piece of our rewards, say fifteen percent of our annual income?" Alina Maretelli, *capo di tutti i capi* of the Cupola and Antonin's aunt, proposes.

"Whoa! What? I mean I don't know how much you all make but fifteen percent is a bit much from our bring-in," TC bursts out.

Devon glares at him until he retakes his seat and shuts his mouth.

"Forgive my adviser, but he has a point. Tell me what you think of this, obuyan. We each take five percent of our last three quarterly bring-in totals and create an Interchange 'pot' so to speak, and we give the organization that the champion is from this sum, or we could give thirty-five percent of the sum to the champion himself and the rest goes to use for preparing the next Interchange."

"Why last three quarterly?" Kazimir asks.

"Well the Interchange is only held every three years so, a quarterly for each year."

"How about five percent of our highest quarterly of each year between Interchanges?" Nishioka requests.

"That's acceptable, so who gets this reward, the organization or the champion and Interchange itself?"

"The champion and Interchange itself," they all say together.

After working this out, Devon petitions to vote for the acceptance of the grand prize for the grand champion. One by one, the bosses place their voting tokens, either 'yes' or 'no' into the jar in the center of the small round table in the middle. Their advisers were seated at high top tables behind each boss. The conditions were unanimously accepted, which was determined to be the only way for the Interchange high council (made up of boss or representative of the five greater organizations—Cupola, Bratva, Yakuza, American Criminal syndicate, and the African syndicate—as well as the reigning champion) to move forward. Following this matter, they discussed other issues late into the night. Devon, as reigning champion, will declare to the whole Interchange, the decision of the prize, and deal with the Garmaggio incident following breakfast in the morning.

Chapter 15

The following morning, Devon walks into the dining commons, flanked by TC and OG, to an ear deafening applause. He sees Hotshot sitting with Bryce Ortega and Dominic Callehann, so he walks over and decides to sit by his son and godchildren. They enjoy a wonderful breakfast, the other organizations waiting for them to eat before getting their own breakfast. After eating and relaxing a little bit, Devon rises and proclaims that it's time to commence the general session of the Interchange. At this command everyone begins to take their dishes to the counter and make their way to the arena which has been converted back into a conference-style hall, with tables surrounding a central stage.

Devon and his cadre of associates took the tables closest to the doors, the delegations of the High Council members took those closest to the stage. Once everyone was seated, Devon, and the other members of the High Council took the stage, and Devon approached the podium.

"Gentlemen, and ladies, welcome to the Interchange. As grand champion, I want to thank you all for attending this inaugural conference and praise your selections as champions, you all fought with honor and glory. To begin this session, I would like to explain what the High Council and I decided would be the rewards of the grand championship melee. First the grand champion is granted a seat on the High Council for his duration as champion, they are also granted the opportunity to join each of our organizations, on the condition that they pass an individual test or trial for each organization. They also stand as the leader for the Interchange, and as such the High Council has determined to grant the champion an advisory committee made up of advisers from each organization within the Interchange, as well as an honor guard comprised of one chosen warrior from each organization. Finally, the High Council has decided that each organization will give five percent of three quarterly reports, the most successful quarterly report for each year between Interchange gatherings. Thirty-five percent of this sum will go to the champion, the rest will be used to finance the next Interchange. Before moving on to other matters, High Council member Kazimir Konstantinavich, Pahkan of the Solntsevskaya Bratva, will present the decision of the High Council regarding Cesare Garmaggio."

Devon takes his seat beside the other High Council members on the stage. Kazimir then stands.

"Thank you, Grand Champion. Due to the nature of the incident following the grand melee, Devon dismissed himself from the discussions regarding the Cupola champion, Cesare Garmaggio. However, it was determined by the High Council that since he was the offended party, he should take the first or final strike," the Pahkan states, revealing an ornate knife. "This knife, provided by Mr. Ortega and Mr. Callehann, will be a symbol of honor and respect, since Cesare Garmaggio violated those ideals, each organizations' lead representative shall strike him with this blade, he shall also be stripped of all membership and honors within any of our organizations, and shown the consequences of his blatant dishonor and disrespect to each of us."

As Kazimir finishes, Bratva guards lead Garmaggio in, flanked by Yakuza and African guards, and escorted by Cupola capos. Once on the stage, he is forced on his knees, shackled to the stage, so he could not retaliate, then Devon approaches the podium.

"I will take the final strike, if it pleases the assembly." Everyone nods.

After proclaiming this, Alina stands, as the Cupola leader she takes the strike that Devon did not, and takes the knife. Before striking him, Alina has him stripped of his shirt and buckets brought forth. Five buckets of ice-cold water, and five buckets of steaming hot water. She has her capos toss a bucket of each on him, cold then hot, until he's soaked and shivering, with hypothermia setting in. The process also made his skin super sensitive to pain. Devon looked in his eyes the whole time, and for the first time since he met Garmaggio, he saw fear and pain overtake the man. Following Alina were the other High Council members, and then Javier Villacres, leader of the Latin American cartels, and Huo Liang, leader of the

Chinese Triad. Lastly, Devon is handed the knife and stands. Before striking him he has Garmaggio unshackled. Garmaggio collapses.

"Stand him up," Devon demands, and the guards obey without hesitation.

Held by the Bratva guards, Devon turns the knife in his hand, examining the wounds that cover his arms, then Devon raises his arm, holds it there for a minute, watching Garmaggio tense up. Devon places his hand on Garmaggio's face and turns it toward his. Garmaggio relaxes and just as he does, Devon strikes him across his chest, then lowers his voice,

"That's for all the pain you caused my family, Colonel!" Devon whispers. "And this is for the pain you caused me." Devon tells the guards to back away, as he jumps, entering a spin kick and kicking Cesare Garmaggio in the jaw.

Devon straightened his suit, placed the knife back on the pillow held by a Cupola operative. He then approaches the podium.

"Gentlemen, and ladies, that man violated every code we hold ourselves too. However, it was because of that code I could not bring myself to strike him chained to the floor. It violates my code of chivalry. The Yakuza have their bushido code, and I have mine. We need to hold ourselves to these standards and those who don't measure up need to be dealt with quickly and quietly, but also very noticeably. I did not know that Alina was going to use the water to induce hypothermia, but I do know that because she did, Cesare Garmaggio will never forget this lesson. You do not violate the codes. You are no longer a boss in America. I'll leave the rest to the respective heads, but as the leader of the American syndicate, I strip you of every title you've held within those borders and to show this I hereby sever the mark of the American Syndicate." At this command, TC brought forth a poker, in a bucket of red-hot coals.

Devon grabbed the poker, TC put the bucket down and turned Garmaggio's wrist, revealing the shield tattoo with two crossed swords with a wolf sitting atop them: the sign of the Gregorian family. Above the shield waved a banner saying *en vino, veritas* and below *lupi simul stare*,- meaning wolves stand together: a family motto. Devon lowered the poker onto the tattoo, making the skin welt and burning the tattoo into a misshaped design, no longer recognizable to the ones TC and the other family members bear.

After giving the poker back to TC, Devon turns back to the other members of the High Council and takes his seat. Kazimir nods to him and rises to the podium.

"As Don Gregory pointed out earlier, as reward for winning the grand championship melee, each organization has to allow him a test to see if he is eligible to join them. I have seen all I need to see from Don Gregory and extend my congratulations to him. I declare Devon Gregory a member of the Solntsevskaya Bratva and thus rank him *Sovet Mudreyshiy*—wisest counsel, the third spy—a title and rank created for and held only by you.

168

Congratulations! If anyone else feels Don Gregory has proven himself enough to join their ranks, please stand."

Alina stands, so does Nishioka, then Abimbola, then Huo Liang, and finally after a few minutes, Javier.

"There you have it, Devon, you've impressed us all. We will adjourn for lunch now, if it please the champion," Kazimir says, looking at Devon, who nods. "And reconvene for the individual ceremonies then before moving into general council discussions."

Chapter 16

Following lunch, everyone reassembled in the arena. Devon held back mentally preparing himself for the initiations. After several minutes the doors open and close. TC and OG have come to collect him. Devon releases a breath he didn't know he'd been holding and removes his blazer, belt, shoes, socks, dress shirt, and undershirt, giving them to Nick who chose to remain outside. Once ready, TC and OG lead him to the doors and open them just wide enough for him to walk through.

On the other side, an aisle had been made, with bosses, underbosses and enforcers of every organization in attendance flanking the path to the stage. Devon strides through, keeping his eyes focused on Kazimir and the other representatives gathered on the stage. Every few feet he was nicked in the arm or chest, but his eyes never diverted, and his face stayed stern. OG and TC remained by the door, each organization placed men on doors to the arena. Devon had finally reached the stage, blood seeping from the cuts. He presents himself to the leaders before kneeling in their presence, bowing his head for a brief second, until he saw them stand. Kazimir approached the podium.

"Fellows of the Interchange, our champion has presented himself to us for rites of entry. Are we all prepared to begin ceremonies for the rites?" A brief period of silence followed. "The High Council has determined the order in which rites are to be issued. Due to the sacred state of our organizations, it has been determined that rites will be given by individual organizations amongst their own leadership. First rites, belong to the Bratva, then Cupola, then Africa, followed by the cartels, the Triad and rites will conclude with the Yakuza. After which our champion will be presented to us and select his committees." Kazimir backs away.

Bryce Ortega approaches the microphone and asks for the Bratva to retire for their rites ceremony. Devon is led out one of the other doors by two Russian brothers, Sergei Pavlovich and Mikkel Gershov. Once surrounded only by Russians, he is led to the center where Kazimir and the spies stand beside a brazier, with a rod protruding from it. Kazimir looks at Devon before stepping back and sitting on a barstool alongside his spies, then nods to his men. Devon realizes what is happening and enters the fetal position before any blows can hit him as the entire assemblage of Russian vory (thieves) attack him. After several minutes, they stop and back away. Devon is pulled to his knees. He looks as Kazimir rises and assesses the 'damage' done.

"I had my vory create an emblem to denote your rank while at lunch and they rushed to find metal, and craft it. However, Andrei is a meticulous craftsman and would not allow it to leave his makeshift forge until he knew it would pass my inspection."

He shows Devon an image of a wolf's head hovering above two intercrossed swords, where the swords meet sits a skull with wings, and around the image is Devon's title among the Vory. Devon nodded and locked eyes with Kazimir as Mikkel and Sergei held him down and one of the spies grabbed the brand, specially shaped to wrap the design on his shoulder. Devon wanted to cry out, to the extent that Kazimir had the other spy hold a wet towel against his mouth to muffle the sound. Devon releases his agitation which, while muffled, still makes everyone in the near vicinity cringe and their ears ring. After completing the brand Kazimir approaches Devon and extends his arm.

"Welcome to Solntsevskaya Bratva, rise *Sovet Mudreyshiy* and join your fellow vory," Kazimir exclaims.

Devon is then attended to, his brand properly wrapped, and he follows everyone back to the arena, walking a few paces behind Kazimir.

Bryce rises again and proclaims the next initiation, the Cupola. Once again Devon is led away.

He is brought to a room where Alina and a few other capos are surrounding a table, on which sits a knife and a gun. Alina looks at Devon as she pricks his finger, which drips onto a picture of Saint Gabriel, patron saint of messengers, Saint Michael, patron saint of warriors, and

Saint Paul, patron saint of writers. After this Alina grabs the pictures, places them in Devon's hand and sets them ablaze. Devon is then explained his duties as a special consigliere in the Cupola as the pictures burn in his hands. Devon juggles the pictures as they burn until they're reduced to pieces the size of dimes. Then Devon returns to the arena.

The African ceremony followed. Devon had to open the jugular of a lion, collect some blood, reseal the wound, and mix the blood with goat's milk. Then drink it. Afterward he was escorted back to the arena. The cartels had him eat the heart of a jaguar. Then he returned to the arena.

The Triad ceremony was interesting. Devon had to kill a Eurasian grey wolf, mix its blood with wine and drink it, and pass beneath an arch of swords reciting oaths the Triad expected him to uphold. Afterward he burns the oaths and raises three fingers on his left hand. He then returns to the arena.

Bryce approaches the mic and announces that the Yakuza can begin their rites. Devon is led away and into a room where he participates in a sakazuki, a symbolic sharing of sake. Afterward Devon is taken to a chair and receives an irezumi tattoo on his arm (opposite the Bratva brand) where the tattoo is done by hand, not a machine. After several hours, they attend to the tattoo to protect it from exposure. Devon then returns to the arena. Devon stands before the assembled crowd and looks among the gathered people, displaying his burns, cuts, and bruises, inflicted upon him during the rites. He then approaches the podium.

"Fellows, I once stood among you as an eager, young, devoted boss, but through hard work and dedication, I've proven myself and now I stand among you not as a boss but as your champion. I've personally told each member of the honor guard and advisers' committee that I selected them, and I would now like each of them to reveal themselves by joining me on stage, the honor guard on my left and the advisers' committee on my right."

Several members of the representative bodies arose and walked toward the stage: Andrei Mendelevich of the Bratva, Akida Tomiji of the Yakuza, Abimbola of the African syndicate, Francesco Batanni of the Cupola, Zhou Lianfou for the Triad, and Jose Gonzalez for the cartels. After they were on stage, another set of individuals arose and joined them, chosen by the honor guard to advise on issues related to the organization. When they were all assembled, each pair, the representatives of each organization, presented Devon with a gift. The Bratva brought forward a specialty weapon, a long staff, one end of which was bladed, the other end heavy, and the staff could be divided into the sword and baton, or used together like a lance. The Yakuza presented him with a specialty kimono, the African syndicate, a traditional African mask, the Cupola, a set of Roman scrolls, the Triad, a traditional tea set, and the cartels brought forth a trained eagle. Devon received each gift before the whole congress.

"With that, I now proclaim the general session of the Interchange open for business. The first matters to be decided are distribution of activities for international purposes. I have consulted with the High Council and we've come up with a preliminary division of activities. These activities will dictate what we can do internationally, within our distinct spheres of influence you are each free to take part in whatever industries you wish. These guidelines apply to when you try to expand into another sector. For instance, the North American sector will be controlled by the Commission who will control the industry of arms trafficking and security racketeering. Within the North American sector, the Commission can have several industries going, but when we try to cross into Europe or Asia, we must stick strictly to arms trafficking and security rackets. The same goes for incoming industries. If the Cupola, for the Mediterranean Sector, tries to expand into North America they must stick to their dictated operation. That way we can minimize the number of international rivalries and stay off Interpol's radar. Therefore, the High Council has reviewed the following and have approved them to be brought before the general assembly. The Commission will control the North American Sector and the arms and securities trafficking industry, the Cupola will control the Mediterranean sector and the theft and fraud industry, the Bratva will maintain control over the European and Near East sector and the gambling and high risk economic activities industry, the Triad will operate the Eastern sector and the human-trafficking industry. The Yakuza will run the Oceania sector and transportation industry, the Africans will run the African and Middle Eastern sector and the white collar and corruption industry, finally, the cartels will maintain the South and Central American sector and the illicit substances industry. Now, each organization can petition the controlling party for permission to enter their sector in a separate industry with the contention that they agree to pay the host organization a dividend no less than twenty percent of the profit margin. Now each leader has a breakdown on the regions within their sector and the description of activities included in their industry. Any concerns and issues can be addressed to my selected adviser who will then refer it to me to discuss with the High Council if it requires such action. Are there any questions about the new procedures? No, OK. I'm instilling a code of confidence into our body. The details of which are outlined in the report you've been given. With that I'd like to lay out the rules for the Interchange. This facility will be maintained by a third party whose name will remain anonymous to avoid unnecessary pressure and stress. You all received the timeline of our meetings. The High Council will meet between those years, here as well, and whenever the reigning grand champion sees fit to assemble them. All other matters having been discussed. I now open the floor to general matters of interest."

After several hours of discussions concerning various topics, Devon concludes the general session and the High

Council does the closing ceremony of the Interchange before dismissing all attendant bodies. Following the meeting everyone went to their designated hangar and left the Swiss safe house.

Chapter 17

Devon had just returned to his home office from a debriefing with the logistics department when his phone rang, he saw a fax was laying on his desk and an email appeared in his inbox. The information contained within didn't surprise him, and he'd been expecting it for quite some time. In fact, he was surprised it hadn't come at the quarterly family meeting a few weeks earlier when they returned from the Interchange summit. Antonin was officially resigning from his position and handing it over to his underboss. Upon seeing the official news however, Devon knew he had to act fast to consolidate with Xavier and Sean before the whole system collapsed. He immediately got on the phone with Xavier and a video conference with Sean.

"Now's the time to expand without conflicting with anyone. The only way this worked was with five bosses who shared a common experience, with Antonin stepping down, we need to act fast to dissolve the Maretelli Mafia and establish our own privatized conglomerate, the Triskelion. The only reason Aaron joined the idea was because he needed the resources, now he has established himself, let's remove our support for him and either take over their combined regions or sell their industries to our international acquaintances," Devon proposes.

"We can't sell it, too much of our income is reliant on those industries," Xavier protests.

"That leaves us one option: conquest. However, the area is too large to select one individual to oversee, which gives us two options moving forward. One. Divide the area and industries between us, or two, we each nominate from our captains and form an oversight team to the area." Sean states.

"Well none of us should spread ourselves out that thin, so let's divide the area between us but leave operations of the area to our underlings we place in the area. They'll come together monthly to ensure that the area is operating correctly, then they'll come to the quarterly meeting on a rotational basis (we'll roll a die when scheduling the meeting and have assigned numbers, whichever the die lands on is whose representative attends). We need to move now though," Devon says.

Within the hour Devon had his local forces deployed to seize operations of all of Jack's distilleries. By employing and backing local competition in his sector, Xavier bought all the properties and used his delegation of security to forcibly evict Jack's underlings in his area, and Sean pulled all his rigs off the contract and used his connections in the industry to stage wrecks into Conway liquor facilities.

Aaron immediately called Devon who denied any type of collaboration between the others. Aaron responded by trying to retaliate but couldn't muster enough forces. Just as Devon was about to break the news to him, several FBI and US marshals barge into his office. Devon hangs up on Aaron and tells Victoria to put him on hold when he calls back.

Devon sits calmly at his desk as the agent in charge approaches.

"Mr. Gregory, you're coming with us," Agent Jacobsen proclaims as two agents walk around the desk.

"Would I be under arrest Special Agent Jacobsen?" Devon asks as he stands.

"Not yet. We're still working on that," Jacobsen says with a smirk.

"Then I'm not going anywhere. Is there anything else I could help you with?"

"Just give us the name of your clients," Jacobsen asks, calling off his men.

"Now I can't do that. They have confidentiality agreements."

"Don't make me call my friends at Interpol and have them come in with the charges of aiding in crimes against humanity and obstructing international justice. You might as well tell us yours, my counterparts in Chicago and Miami already got the lists from Mr. Jones and Mr. Gallagher." Jacobsen grins and stands triumphantly.

"Wow, that was easier said than done. You just broke the number one rule of law enforcement, you revealed your hand. I happen to know that you just lied to the leading supplier of your equipment and that of the US military. However, we can reconcile from this little mess and I won't tell the director and POTUS that you just disarmed the nation."

"How so?" Agent Jacobsen adjusts his stance and changes his tone entirely, dismissing all the other agents besides his two advisers, one from marshals and the other from the FBI.

"I can just happen to give you the name of the largest smuggler of bootlegged alcohol on the west coast as well as an entire dossier of corrupt government employees nationwide with proof to support it. All this in exchange for your solemn commitment before these witnesses and God that you'll leave my associates and I alone for half a decade. What do you say?"

"Fair enough. What's the name?" Jacobsen says shaking Devon's hand and signing a breach of contract form for the release of information.

"Aaron Jacobs! Good day Special Agent Jacobsen. Travis and Conner will see you out. Thank you for your cooperation."

"Thank you for yours," Jacobsen says, leaving the room thinking he was triumphant.

Devon sits back at his desk, calls Aaron and tells him that the issue will be resolved shortly and that he's sorry for the confusion. He then conferences Sean and Xavier and fills them in on the details of the deal. Both of whom confirm that FBI and marshals just left their offices following short phone calls. They then discuss the policy and procedural changes to set up the Triskelion. The call ends as the sun sets.

Devon walks over to the bank of windows flanking his and Victoria's penthouse apartment. Nick hands him a glass of scotch before being called upstairs by his mother to help with putting his twin siblings to sleep. Devon walks out onto the balcony overlooking the city and takes a deep breath, enjoying the view of HIS city held with an iron grip and watched with steel eyes.

Chapter 18

Four years have elapsed since Devon Gregory successfully evaded the prying eyes of the Federal government, one that he once thought secure. When it turned out that things were not as they seemed, and once the problems in his new territories settled down, Devon turned his eyes onto them and started investigating his clients who held office in Washington DC. To do this, Devon limited available forces for some, and limited supply shipments for others. Through these channels and renegotiations, Devon was able to learn that certain individuals in the controlling offices of several major operations were collaborating to expose and remove themselves from Devon's grip. This order within the government sought to coordinate policies through their connections, however Devon and his forces were able to contain the spread of their agenda. After discovering all this Devon created a Special Operations division within Triskelion Security answerable only to him and led by none other than Nick Gregory himself.

Within several months the order was ousted from their positions within the government. However, having become obsessed with routing the order, Devon's national empire was crumbling. Captains of neighboring sectors were going to war and formulating criminal families and enterprises on their own, without Devon's oversight the empire was functioning but not excelling. The commission still controlled the Interchange, but Devon was not the victor. Marcus Fonte, Sean's lead caporegime, had won the melee and maintained interests. This shift in control however was systemic.

En Vino Veritas,
Having realized the risk we're taking staying off radar far outweighs the risk of actual running our operations, we've decided to retire ourselves from the criminal underworld. We've each met with our capos and determined who is leaving with us and who is staying and have nominated our selections to take over in our stead. Those lists are contained within.
Lupi simul stare,
Snakes and Bullet.

Nick walks into his father's office with a print out of the email that just came through.

Devon is staring at the large video screen he had installed in his office when he created the Special Operations division. As his son reads the letter he slides depictions of forces around the screen displaying a map of the nation. When Devon finishes he turns to his son and asks, "Is that all?"

"Well there's also this." Nick picks up the remote off the low bookcase beneath the monitor and flips to the news simul broadcast screen, displaying several news programs at once all running the same story.

Governor Antonin Maretelli has just won the final debate in the presidential election, thousands from across the nation and world have gathered this evening in Tucson to hear the governor's remarks on this glorious occasion. Governor Maretelli has now won all three presidential debates and polling shows that he has an eighty-three point four percent approval rating across the board. Strong Republicans and strong Democrats were seen in the audience of supporters of the governor, who is the first major third party candidate to get this far into an election with odds looking favorable. Is this the end of the two-party system that's dominated US politics for one hundred and fifty years?

"We need to deal with both these issues and fast, sir," Nick proclaims to his father.

"We already have. I just finished sending out orders of deployment for teams to dominate both Sean's territories and Xavier's. I also sent a delegation to Tucson to throw our support behind Antonin and got off the phone with Kazimir not thirty minutes ago who tells me the former high councilors are reaching out to their legitimate contacts to throw their support behind him as well. They also ordered their local organizations to coordinate with our offices nationwide to quell and suppress any major dissenters of our control."

"Well OK then. Is there anything else you need from me then or should I return to my office and coordinate with Marcus on our operations on that side of things?"

"Return to your office. Tell Marcus I said hello and we'll go from... Hello Agent Jacobsen."

The doors to his office fly open and in struts the overzealous special agent who tried to arrest him several years ago. The agent places a device on the desk and hits a button the device hums loudly.

"Morning, Mr. Gregory, this is to unofficially warn you that tomorrow the FBI will officially open another investigation into your company due to the chatter that says your two associates are moving into retirement and that you'll be expanding your operation. The Oval Office wants a large win on crime before the end of the election so they're running down every possible lead no matter how slim. And your file is not that." He turns off the device and heads to the door.

"Thank you, Henry, please give my best to Cindy and the kids."

"And to you Devon! Nick, Good day."

Devon leans up in his chair and gets on the phone while Nick rushes out of the office. They hand control of the empire to former staff sergeant Jonathan Markovich who was one of Devon's most trusted capos. He was slated to become the enforcer when Devon left and the upper echelon of the organization move into their new roles, but plans were changing. They then print all files and have their computers wiped of all illicit activity while they have the paper copies transported to the old facility to be used as Jonathan's base of operations, where the files were be placed on a chopper and taken to the Swiss Alps office, not too far from the resort where the Interchange conferences are hosted.

With all situations under control on that end, Devon turns back to running the legitimate side of his business, contacting regional overseers for all their contracts nationwide. While the Gregorian family can't roam borders with security and weapons, Triskelion Security is the top supplier of privatized military and the leading arms manufacturer in the Northern Hemisphere.

Throughout the day, the letter from Sean and Xavier nagged at him and slowly he began to realize they were correct.

Chapter 19

Several months later, Devon is escorted from the Presidential Suite at The Jefferson to the Quill Cocktail Lounge. Seated at the bar is James Callehann.

"Devon, are you sure about this?" James asks, sliding a card toward him but not letting go just yet.

"Absolutely. Victoria and I want to have what you and Cynthia do." Devon answers, placing his hand on the card.

"No you don't." James states absently before returning to the issue at hand, "All right. Poplar Cabinet seven fifteen sharp. Tell Agent Trent to remember he's not just Secret Service, he's a Trent."

That night, Devon follows James' directions and is granted an audience with the president. Devon gives him the files on two hundred and fifty of the worst criminals in Triskelion's US contracts. After comparing the cost of forfeiting the contracts versus the risk of the entire company going under, the board of directors permitted Devon to release the files to the correct agency. Devon then asked James to set up a meeting with the president and the National Security Council.

The conditions of getting full unredacted access to the remaining Triskelion contracts was that they limit the scope of their investigation and that any files requested have to be approved by a co-operative task-force of Triskelion and government agencies. Devon leaves the meeting victorious.

By November 5th, The president got his crackdown on crime and the family had survived the investigation. Although most of their industries were in shambles, their two major ones, security and arms control, were still intact. Having realized that his friends made the correct move when the time was right and with a target now on his back, Devon slowly began to distance himself from the criminal underworld.

Then, on November 18th, He called a press conference and revealed on national television that Triskelion Security and himself had been involved in the criminal underworld for about twenty years.

"Although founded on the idea of safety and security for all, Triskelion Security, under my guidance was propelled to success by taking contracts with clientele who are known associates of various organizations in the criminal underworld. While these men are known criminals, the contracts made with them are perfectly legal and will withstand any scrutiny of the law. The underlying cause of this extra-legal nature of contracts lies in our non-disclosure agreement clause, which affirms that no communication will be conducted about what actions or events the involved parties are subject to. I couldn't even tell you who was on which detail, much less what they did. All I know is who to contact and where they could be found in case of emergencies. By doing this I was able to immunize myself and my fellow top-level bureaucrats of this company from all legal actions taken out against my officers. This does not excuse whatever they may or may not have done, but I will vouch for every one of my men because when they signed on with this company, they signed a document that states that they could and would deny any service requested of them that they found to have 'crossed the line'. That point for each person is different, but I will guarantee that all my officers performed to the best of their ability always. Having said that, and with that in mind, I called you all here to reveal this to you and to open our doors, and our books to all scrutiny. The board of directors, trustees, and shareholders, have all pledged to turn away from the illicit activity we were once involved in as a company, but we will retain our legitimate business. With over two thousand five hundred contracts worldwide for security and fifteen hundred orders for arms, we are rebranding ourselves Triskelion Security, Armor, and Arms Manufacturing. Thank you and good day," Devon says to the gathered press outside his building before stepping away from the podium.

"At this time we will take questions. However, all questions pertaining to our contacts within the criminal hierarchy of the nation and the world will not be accepted and will be skipped. Persistence, while admirable, on this issue will be met with equal force, up to and including removal of your press pass with us, and/or being barred from the property. Please respect our wishes on these issues and I will be happy to answer any questions you have," TC says having stepped up to the podium.

Volley after volley of questions arose. Most were bordering the line established about connections to the criminal underworld, while some were ignored, most were answered with full transparency. Afterward Devon, TC, and Conner returned to the conference room and overlooked the city without the stress of what lies beneath pressing down on them.

Epilogue

MAFIA MAGNATE NAMED NATIONAL POLICE COMMISSIONER. In the wake of his presidency, Antonin Maretelli made headlines internationally as he not only privatized the police force of the United States but put at its helm former colonel, Devon Gregory. Several months ago, Gregory revealed to the nation that his company, Triskelion Security, had risen to prominence on the heels of crime with Gregory himself being associated with international criminal organizations across the world. Despite this revelation, or perhaps because of it, Devon Gregory's nomination was swiftly accepted and he was duly sworn in by the president this morning. Also in attendance were vice president, Aaron Jacobs, along with several members of the cabinet and Gregory's family. In other news, the stocks of the Interchange Resort Hotel and Spa facility in the Swiss Alps is still on the rise...

Devon turns off the television as the chopper glides over France, heading to the first of many dinners to come with his 'family'. Bryce Ortega, Dominic Callehann, Nick Gregory, Zander Jones and Logan Gallagher had all managed to talk to Dominic's father and obtain ownership of the Swiss Alps location, which they quickly turned into a high end resort and spa. Logan oversees flights and transportation around the resort, much like his father does, Zander runs the variety of entertainment locations draped across the property, Nick of course coordinates security, Bryce manages the facilities and Dominic oversees guest services.

As the chopper lands on the tarmac, a young lad approaches with a step stool. Devon gets out, followed by Victoria, Daniel, Charlotte, and the two toddler twins. The family is escorted inside and led to a grand suite. After freshening up, Devon kisses Victoria, who is lounging about reading a book while the toddlers play in the bath, and Daniel and Charlotte are 'exploring' the place they visit several times a year now.

"I'm headed out, babe, don't wait up. I can't control myself if you do and we don't need a sixth," Devon says gesturing to the bathroom.

Victoria chuckles and playfully slaps her husband. Things have gotten so much more relaxed since Devon released the secrets of Triskelion. For a while there it was difficult, him being called away several hundred times in the night to address the issue with some foreign mafioso. However, that stopped when Kazimir visited and applauded Devon, and released him from his obligations to the Bratva, and the Interchange.

Devon heads out of the room and goes up the elevator to the secret pavilion located atop the main hotel of the resort. He gets off the elevator, slides on slippers, puts a smoking robe on and enters the pavilion. Standing within the room were Sean and Logan, Xavier and Zander, Nick, James Callehann and Dominic, Lucian Ortega and Bryce, all of whom were chatting. Then Devon glanced to the table where they were normally playing poker and smoking cigars. In the dark, lit only by light from the sconces nearby and the small dim overhead chandelier, sat Kazimir Konstantinavich and behind him stood his son, Dmitri.

"Hello old friend, it's been a while since we last saw each other. You remember Dmitri, yes?" Kazimir says gesturing for Devon to join him at the table.

"Of course, he was but ten when we first met, right? Now look at him, a specimen of manliness. Has he joined the brotherhood?"

"Oh no, I took a page from your book and pulled out of the game. My son has luckily not followed in my footsteps. In fact it is for him that I am here."

"Very well what do you need?"

"An endorsement, and a favor. Dmitri is running for office in Moscow, and he's set to win but your vote of confidence and of your connections would ensure his success."

"Of course, he has my support. Now what is this favor?"

"A child, children really. Dmitri and his brother were having too good of a time one night and got several women pregnant while out. They're all expecting soon. I'm using my remaining contacts to get them safe passage to New York. Can you help find them a place to stay and raise the children?"

"I think I know a guy who knows a guy that can help," Devon says smiling and pulling out his phone.

"Good. Then let the festivities begin and I will get out of here," Kazimir says.

"Why leave? We've got premium streaks, Cuban cigars and loads of stories to tell and hear. Please stay and join us," Devon offers.

Kazimir thinks it over before joining them at the table where the others filled in after the meeting was over. The boys had women carrying trays of steaks and cigars out as the men set up for the first of many rounds of poker.

Before things got too crazy, Devon rose from the table for a toast.

"Gentlemen, may this be the start of a tradition that spans several generations. Although for a different purpose, it still rings true in this situation. Say it with me fellas."

Devon declares the full Gregorian family motto, looking to TC and Conner who had just walked into the pavilion, "Wolves forever stand together, may truth and justice prevail."